What Hop

The story continues on Star Gazer Island. Three women find friendship and courage on the shores of Corpus Christi Bay. Come visit the Star Gazer Inn, with a side trip to the McIntyre Ranch, as widow Alice McIntyre finds her way between two worlds.

The Star Gazer Inn is packed as the summer nights cool off, but temperatures are rising as Alice and Seth are exploring a new level of their "friendship" and both are nervous.

Oh, the "glamping" we will do...Riley has more than he bargained for as the venue opens, and the women show up in droves, ready to be pampered while roughing it on the ranch's beach-side retreat. And the woman he's been hoping he would find just pulled into the park.

Jackson and Nina are expecting...puppies!

And Lisa is not happy when an old flame shows up as a guest at the inn.

Put your feet up and grab a glass of sweet iced tea or a glass of your favorite wine. This new series follows Alice, her sons, and her friends—and new loves—on the South Texas coast, with its sparkling topaz water. You'll want to dip your toes in and stay awhile.

WHAT HOPES ARE MADE OF

Star Gazer Inn of Corpus Christi Bay, Book Three

DEBRA CLOPTON

What Hopes are Made of

Copyright © 2020 Debra Clopton Parks

CHAPTER ONE

Alice McIntyre stood beside her son Riley. She was amazed at what he'd done for the last several months here on the beach property their ranch owned. He had gotten the desire to set up the beach and the land next to the beach as a campground. And she loved the idea. It was a sizeable area that had been unused for a long time.

She turned to smile at him. "It's going to be great, Riley. When you and your three brothers were kids, I loved it when we would all come here and camp out. Your dad enjoyed spending that time with you boys. And I loved watching him teaching all four of you how to swim and fish from this shore." William had loved being here with her and their sons. She'd loved watching them together here, and not just on the ranch.

"I have fond memories of those times with you and Dad. Too bad as we got older, we were all too busy on the ranch to take much time off to come here. Instead, we went to the public beaches with our friends when we had time. And then Dad drowned in the river, riding his horse across, and we lost him… While I've been out here working lately, he's been on my mind."

"He would love what you're doing. But, he also understood you teenagers wanting to be on the regular beach and be around pretty girls and your friends."

"I know. But no matter what, I will always regret losing him. Getting this camping program set up has been a little complicated, but I've enjoyed it. I'll have programs for regular campers but will also specialize in holding three or four days of camping for large groups of ladies. That's why the large tents for special events will be put up, for evening gatherings with dinner and music. Massages, body masks, manicures, and morning exercise…all kinds of things will be offered. Whatever the ladies request and are willing to pay for will be done."

"Interesting. And only for ladies?"

"That's right. Ladies' camping groups are doing well. If a good-sized group comes in, then the cost is going to be reasonable as it's divided between everyone. They don't get charged too large of a fee. So, I believe it will do really well. And by the time it opens up next weekend, I'll be past ready. The first weekend of April will be nice—not too hot and not too cold. But it will be regular family camping to start."

"I think it's all a great idea. I'm going to have to come and stay out here at least one weekend when it's women only, just to experience it. The massages and mud baths sound great. And manicures—all of that good stuff sounds very interesting to get done on a camping trip. What do they call it?"

Riley grinned. "Glamping. But there are all kinds of glamping, some far fancier than others. Since mine is on a beach, and I'm not certain how popular it will be out here, I'm starting off small. I'm focusing on family gatherings for two weeks of a month, but will book glamping weekends for large groups of women

3

who want to enjoy the beach, sunsets, stargazing, and watching the rising sun. Then the glamour comes in: enjoyable meals, music, and pampering."

"I'm in. It sounds wonderful. How did you get this great idea?"

"It got my attention when I stopped at a gas station last summer and talked to a woman pulling a small camper. She'd just spent the weekend at a glamping gathering with her camping group."

"I remember you telling me about the lady pulling a small camping trailer."

"I did. Her camper had Live, Laugh, Love and Enjoy Life… It's just too dang short."

"I love that brilliant advice." Alice smiled at her son, feeling in her heart that the woman had gotten him interested in her in those few moments. The woman hadn't told Riley her name—they hadn't talked long—but he'd been obsessed with opening up a glamping camp ever since. This was the first time he mentioned the lady to Alice again. He had concentrated on getting this place finished. She couldn't help feeling that he would see this nameless woman again, at the very glamping spot they looked at. And Alice liked the idea.

"I guess I better head back to the inn. But I really love this. I'll be eager to see how everyone enjoys it. Most especially this glamping part."

He put his arm around her shoulders as they walked to her small Mercedes. "I'm glad you came out. I'm going to come to the inn for dinner Friday night."

"Really!" Alice looked up at him. "It will be great to see you there. Are you meeting someone, bringing a date?"

"I'm meeting Tucker for dinner. He's been helping me when he has time. Which hasn't been as much as he thought since our newlywed brother Jackson has booked several sales on the ranch. And since he's in charge of the cattle, Tucker has been occupied with that. We've both been busy, so we decided we'd have dinner together at the inn on Friday."

"Wonderful. I'll be there, and it will be nice to see both of you."

"Good to hear. How are you doing?" he asked as

she sank into the driver's seat.

She smiled up at him. "We're doing great. The Star Gazer Inn is doing well, staying semi-booked, and the restaurant is a success. Locals love it, and people drive from Corpus Christi and enjoy a meal there."

"That's good. How are you doing personally?"

Of course, he was asking about her and Seth. Just the thought of Seth sent a tingling wave of happiness through her. "Since Jackson and Nina got married, Seth and I have gone out there for dinner a couple of times. And also, out on his boat too. Fun."

Riley grinned and his eyes twinkled. "Good. From what I've heard from everybody, you are spending a lot of your time off, which isn't much, with Seth. I think he's a great man. You seem happy and I'm glad."

"I am, Riley. Okay, I'm gone. See you Friday."

He closed the door and waved as she drove down the road toward the gate. He seemed really happy that she was happy. She had loved his dad with all her heart, and she believed all of her sons were glad she was in a growing relationship with Seth.

She was in love with Seth, and she believed they would all be happy for her. She just had to adjust to it herself.

Sophie Regan closed her laptop computer, very glad to have finished another land appraisal before Friday. She was now free for a long weekend. Her appraisal business gave her freedom to book her own schedule of work and time off, working from her home office. It kept her really busy, but only at the rate she wanted. She controlled her workplace and had no desire to ever work inside a large office again.

Sophie rose from her desk chair, strode out of her office and into the kitchen for a glass of tea. She walked out onto the back porch and breathed in the spring air. She loved spring and smiled out over the ocean—which she also loved. Even though she wasn't on the beach, this apartment had a terrific second-story view, overlooking Corpus Christi Bay. And for what she did with her appraisals, she had a central location to reach anywhere in the area.

She took a drink of her tea, then sank into one of her two outdoor chairs. Her thoughts went to the new campground she'd just learned about. It was close across the bay, near the cute town of Star Gazer Island. She'd been there a few times on her way to do land appraisals near the area and had enjoyed it. So much that she'd even considered moving there, but then thought it might put her too far out of reach for the primary banks who used her before a sale. Or of ranch owners who wanted new appraisals of their own. Here, her name was well enough known that she didn't have to rent an office or have a sign to get enough business to support her and her retirement account. Not that at thirty she was anywhere near retiring.

It enabled her, as a single female, to control her time and do what she enjoyed. So Friday—tomorrow—morning, she was driving out to look at the newly opening campground. She hoped it was an ideal place to book for her camping group at the end of the month. The campgrounds she'd booked had canceled abruptly when it had sold to a hotel chain. She'd ignored a statement that it could happen, thinking it wouldn't affect her and her group.

Wrong—it did. But it was a perfect opportunity to get out of town alone and check out the new camp. She booked herself a couple of nights at Star Gazer Inn and was looking forward to seeing it. The inn had reopened last summer around this time, and from everything she'd heard, it was an amazing beach inn, with a great restaurant connected to it. This was going to be an interesting and relaxing weekend.

The next morning, Sophie was up early and on the road toward Star Gazer Island and the camp she was eager to see. She was always excited to get her research done, and she needed to act quickly on this cancelation's rebooking. She drove across the bridge on Texas 361, enjoying the ocean view of the long island that stretched along the coast. The windows were rolled down, letting the sound of the ocean inside the Jeep.

She had looked up the owner of the new camp and found Riley McIntyre was opening it. McIntyre was the last name of a wealthy ranch family out here in this area, and he was one of them. He obviously didn't need the income of the camp but must enjoy camping.

She thought about the cowboy she met last summer who had helped wash her windshield and fill her tank up. She'd been coming back from a camping trip with her camping trailer. He'd asked questions, and she'd told him about the glamping that she loved.

She also had seen the interest in the man's eyes, not just in her but in glamping. But she had no idea who he was; she'd been in a rush to get home and hadn't asked his name, and he hadn't asked hers. The last thing she wanted was to meet a stranger at a gas station and then find out she should have gotten into her car and drove away.

It was close to ten o'clock by the time she arrived at the beautiful Star Gazer Inn, sparkling in the morning sunshine. She smiled and couldn't wait to see inside. This was going to be a wonderful weekend, no matter what happened with the camp.

CHAPTER TWO

The wind was warmer than it had been on their last trip, because spring was here. She looked at Seth and of course, as always, her heart jumped. She was thoroughly happy to be around him at the moment—at any moment, actually.

From the first day Seth had arrived to give her a bid on the remodeling of the inn, she had been attracted to him. Which was startling, because she hadn't felt that way since she'd fallen in love with William and married him. He'd passed away, but her love for him would always be alive.

Then she'd met Seth. It wasn't until about the end of his remodeling the inn that she had admitted that she wanted to date him. As a widow, she hadn't wanted to jump into a relationship too quickly. So, they'd become friends, and he'd taken her out on this wonderful boat, and he hadn't pushed her at all. Finally, she admitted she was serious about what she felt toward him. But she'd also told him she had a new business; she had sons who were finally getting married, and she didn't want to rush into a relationship. He had been totally understanding, considering he'd been through losing his wife a couple of years before she lost William.

Now they were more serious and committed to each other. She loved him and he loved her, and she knew he would marry her the moment she was ready. The very idea had her grinning.

He looked over at her now and smiled. "What are you thinking about? It looks like you're enjoying it with all that grinning that you're doing."

She laughed. "I was just thinking about you and about us and our relationship. It was a very busy week at the inn, but I was looking very much toward spending today with you. And I know I haven't seen you that much this week because you have been really busy too."

"I am very busy on my current house remodeling job. But I wouldn't mind a call from you anytime you want to do it. I'm glad we're out here today and that you can relax."

She sat back in the boat's chair. "So, are you enjoying the project you're doing?"

"I am. It's not your inn, which, as you know, I enjoyed above anything I've ever done, and I met the nicest person at that inn who changed my life." He held out his arm; she stood and stepped up next to him. He wrapped the arm around her waist and drove the boat with his other hand.

She leaned her head against his shoulder. "And I can say the same for you."

He tugged her closer and kissed the top of her head. "Like I've told you before, I would have waited for you to fall in love with me as long as it took, and I enjoy every moment we spend together."

He slowed the boat along the coast of Star Gazer Island, then he pulled the throttle back and turned off the engine. Then he wrapped both arms around her. They always enjoyed standing here like this, on the horizon of the ocean together.

Looking up at him, she knew she wanted to marry him. But he had promised to give them time, just like she wanted. When she looked into his eyes, she knew she was getting closer to not putting it off any longer.

But he was very busy right now, and she had to let him finish this big job first. Because she had a feeling that when she said she was ready, he would want to marry her right then.

He leaned down in that moment and kissed her, and she melted against him.

* * *

The young receptionist at the front desk checked Sophie into the inn and gave her the room key. The inn was just beautiful. Sophie had taken her things to her room, gazed out the window at the beautiful grounds below, and then out at the beach and ocean...all was amazing. She grabbed her key and hurried down to the beach for a quick look, then headed back to her Jeep and headed out to find the campgrounds.

Twenty minutes later, she turned in to the drive where a McIntyre Camp sign was being hung by a cowboy on a ladder. As she parked, got out of the Jeep and then stepped forward, the cowboy smiled. Something about him was familiar.

He pushed his hat back, exposing his eyes.

She halted, shocked. "It's you."

"Yes, and it's you. It's been about a year since I saw you at the gas station." He climbed from the ladder, his smile wider now. "I'm Riley McIntyre, and this is actually part of the McIntyre Ranch. And you are?" He held his hand out to her.

She placed her hand in his, loving the feel of his rough hand and the smile on his face. "I'm Sophie Regan. I book the camping trips for my group, 'Glamping We Shall Do', and I need a rebooking by the end of April, so I'm checking this place out. Will it be open by then and willing to take a single, private group."

Looking startled, he put his hand on his hip.

15

"Actually, it opens next weekend, the first weekend of April."

"Do you run it? Or lease it out to a company that runs it?"

"I run it. I'll be happy to show you around. After I met you that day at the gas station and you talked about your weekend camping group, it got me intrigued. I'm telling you, once I investigated the topic of glamping, I was driven to learn more. After that, I started getting this camp planned out and then did a few ads for the first few weekends open to anyone. The glamping weekends are on the list to get set up."

"That's awesome. And I'm honestly glad to find you here. I can tell you are very interested in making this a great place."

"Until I met you, it never occurred to me, but then I couldn't stop thinking about it. We have this huge section of beach here on our ranch, and I thought it would be a cool thing to try. I've got families booked for the first two weekends of camping, hanging out and playing on the beach together. But the glamping ads will go out later, maybe next week if this first regular weekend goes well. I was hoping May might be the first booking for glamping. Now, you've showed up, which is terrific, it will be April. I'm probably going to ask you a lot of questions while we walk around here."

She smiled. Now she was looking forward to this weekend a lot more than she had even imagined. "You can ask me all the questions you want. And I have some for you."

"Anything you need to know, ask. I'll be happy to help. Now, just hop in your Jeep and follow me in."

"Perfect." With that, she strode back to her Jeep and climbed in. By that time, he was in his truck, leading the way through the gate. Riley was her cowboy from the gas station last summer—it was hard to believe. And exciting.

When they arrived at the campgrounds, she parked beside him. Then she climbed out of her Jeep and stared at the beautiful sand and ocean that she could see over the sandy hills. It was, in some ways, similar to what had been at the Star Gazer Inn.

"It's beautiful." She spun from the water and found him watching her.

"I think so. It's a great place to camp, isn't it, with the open view of the ocean? It's a pretty beach. And at night, with the moon shining, it's gorgeous, too. I've had this expansive grass area set up for camp trailers and then had restrooms built over there." He pointed to a nice-looking brick building.

"Can we walk over there and look at those? See, in my group, it's all women. Average age is thirty to sixty—young and old women. Some haven't been married in years, some divorced, some who've never been married, and some who are married but enjoy time spent with girlfriends. Anyway, all women, so a nice restroom would be great."

"I tried to do it right. In all honesty, after I had that conversation with you, I started researching that week. Women like nice things, so I tried to have the bathroom designed to appeal to them."

"I think that's really cool." When they reached the bathrooms, she entered immediately, and he stood at the door.

"What do you think?" he asked.

She couldn't even speak for a moment. It was so well done, and big. There were ten restroom stalls, and across the room, ten changing rooms each beside a shower. And a section of sinks with enormous mirrors at the front of the building. Down the middle of the room was a long bench. The room was painted pale peach and an amazing painting of a beautiful beach, ocean, and softly clouded sky hung on the wall at the wall between the entrance and the exit.

"It's beautiful. Did you pick out these colors and the design? And I love that picture."

"I came up with what I thought I would like, and then I got the opinion of my mom and my two sisters-in-law. These were the winners. My sister-in-law Nina is an artist, and she donated the picture. I tried my hardest to buy it, but finally gave up and accepted her gift."

"She is a fantastic artist, and obviously generous too."

"Yes, she is both. I like the room, and your reaction assured me I made the right decisions."

She smiled at him. "I'm very glad that I could help in some way."

"You did, very much. Do you want to see the mens restroom? It's basically the same, but a bit bolder and no picture."

"I'm sure it's great, but since I have no male campers, I'd rather go look at where you're going to put the camping trailers. And everything else that will make the ladies smile…facials and massages—you know, all that good fun stuff."

"Let's go." He grinned, causing her pulse to race.

She wasn't sure when she had reacted to a man like she was reacting to Riley. She wasn't complaining at all. She was both cautious and excited about the feeling.

They walked together over toward an area that was freshly concreted.

"This slab is for a party area and will be covered with a large tent top, have tables and chairs and an area to dance, if they wanted to. I know it's all women, but from what I read, sometimes groups of women just want to dance as a group and have fun. Over there will be additional tent camping." He pointed to the marked-off sections, with picnic tables, fire pits, and water stations.

"I think that would work great. And you've got that—I guess that's an eating place right there, that cute little colorful building?"

"Correct. There will be tables and seats on the surrounding sand. It will do breakfast items and lunch and certain dinner meals that are paid for as people order them. But special dinners will have to be hired and brought in. You choose what you'd like to have, and it's figured into your camp charge and paid ahead. Do you have any suggestions for a group of women like yours?"

"We like junk sometimes and sometimes we like salads. But we don't always book our meetings at really fancy places that have our meals. They can bring their own meals in their campers if they prefer, and I'll decide what's for supper after I know what the choices are for Friday and Saturday evenings. Will that work?"

Startled, he stared at her. "So, you're actually booking my new camp for your camping session?"

"Yes. I am. It's a beautiful beach. The women will love it. You're setting everything up to make a comfortable weekend for the ladies. We had our camp booked at the end of the month and it got canceled last week because the camp sold to a hotel group. Everyone got alerted that their plans were changed.

Oddly, I saw your ad for campers and group glamping weekends coming soon. Instantly, I had to come check it out. I had no idea it was you."

"I'm thrilled you saw the ad. How many women do you usually have?"

"Anywhere from thirty to sometimes sixty-something. That's about as much as I can handle. This is our first meeting of the year, and we have fifty-five women booked. But I have to make sure they can all still come. Some might not because the Corpus area is farther away from the Galveston camp that had been set for the last weekend of April. Does that date work? I understand if it isn't available."

"I have not booked that weekend. And it's perfect timing, since I wanted a few weeks before I had the first glamping gathering. Give us time to come up with everything you want and my workers in the food booth to get settled in, too."

She smiled, so relieved. "Wonderful. Can I take a few pictures to share in my email to the ladies?"

"Sure. Anything you want. You've made my day."

She looked at his gorgeous brown eyes. "And you've made mine."

CHAPTER THREE

Riley watched as Sophie took pictures of the area. He was still getting over the fact that she was actually here. He had just gotten the place almost ready, and she had shown up, booked her camp, and was bringing her group at the end of the month. It felt like it was meant to be, because she was the one who had gotten him interested in glamping in the first place. And she had now booked the first one.

He was thrilled. "Are you staying on Star Gazer Island for the weekend?"

"Yes, at the amazing Star Gazer Inn. I can't wait to explore it more when I get back."

He let out a chuckle. "My mom's place. You did

right. It's an amazing inn."

She lowered her phone as she gaped at him. "Seriously, your mom owns it? I had no idea."

"She does. And she loves it. She loved remodeling it, too. She must not have been there if you already checked in. She enjoys talking to new company."

"I was checked in by a young lady. But I would have loved meeting your mother."

"She actually lives at the inn, so I'm sure you will. She'd have asked you what brought you to town if you had met her and when you said this camp, she would have told you I was her son."

"Certainly, she would have. Both this and the inn are beautiful places to be proud of." She smiled warmly, her eyes twinkling. "I'll look forward to meeting your mother. It's been a long time since I had a job over in this direction, so I took this opportunity to come see it. I stayed at inn a couple of times about six or seven years ago. Sadly, it closed not long after that, and it is wonderful that it's open again."

"I'm already sure you're going to enjoy your afternoon and evening there. Did you eat lunch before you came out here?"

"No. I had eaten a late breakfast, so I checked in, then went out to look around at the beautiful garden and the beach. Then, I came on out to see this awesome place, hoping someone would be here."

"I'm glad I was here. I have done a lot of work myself and Tucker, my brother, has helped a few times. He's in charge of the cattle at the ranch. He didn't get to help as much as he thought because of work at the ranch, even though he was interested in the camp. My other brother, Jackson, manages the business side of the ranch—sales and auctions—and all that kept him busy. He would have been here today, but he's at the ranch making sure that the cattle are all ready for the sale set up for tomorrow evening. I'll be there too."

"Really? So you not only do this, you work at your family's ranch, too?"

"Well, I did, but I've been focusing on the camp. We have plenty of cowboys on the ranch, so Tucker and Jackson were fine with me doing this. They're the older brothers and the lead positions they carry fits them. I'm the youngest of four. I love ranching but also get bored, and they all know it. My brother, Dallas, who was a champion bull rider, is now married and running his bride's ranch and the new business they started together, raising their own cattle and horses. He's loving running his own place with his new bride. Me, I needed something new too, and when we ran into each other at the gas station that day, my interest was hooked. But I'll be at the ranch sale tomorrow night to support the cattle sale."

"McIntyre Ranch has a wonderful reputation. But I'm glad you are interested in this camp."

He loved her smile and got one at that moment. She was beautiful and her glossy red hair and her pretty green eyes were amazing. His smile broadened.

"Why do you smile every time you look at me?" she asked.

"Well, for one, you're beautiful and two, I'm really glad you showed up. I didn't know your name when I met you at the gas station. I didn't know where you lived. I didn't know if you traveled a long way to wherever you had been camping out. I've thought about you a couple times while working on this. Okay, a few more times than that, because it was obvious you loved glamping."

"Very true." She grinned.

"To be honest, and I hope you don't take it wrong, I thought there might be a slight chance that if I opened this, you'd show up and I'd finally know your name."

"Wow, I had no idea."

"You inspired me to do this, although you didn't know you did, but also I really wanted to know your name and get to know you. I hope that doesn't sound bad to you."

"Um, no. It's nice because I have actually thought about you a couple of times, too, and I had no idea coming here, that this is where you'd be. Absolutely no idea, but I'm glad. Now, I don't want to keep you from doing what you need to do, so I'll head back to the inn. Is there anything you need to discuss with me about it? I mean, I've got time tonight—after you finish what you were doing this afternoon—so if you need me for anything, you know where to find me. Or I can give you my phone number."

"What do you say if I go home and grab the paperwork and meet you at the inn this evening for dinner?"

"Great. I mean, that would actually be perfect. I'll go enjoy the rest of the afternoon on the beach area and send some of my people a text to get their reaction. I think they will have a great response. I can tell you about it and then we can talk about things they would like."

"That sounds perfect. I'll show up about six-thirty. Does that work?"

"Yes, it does. Thanks. I came here, hoping that it would be great and that I could book a weekend, but I had no idea it would be this great. Well, if we can afford it. Hopefully, I can tell you to charge more because you're charging too little."

He laughed. "If I quote a number that's over what you think is right, then I'll learn something. But I think from all the comparisons that I've done that you'll be happy."

"Perfect." She headed to her Jeep and opened her door before he could reach around her to get to the handle. Then, she scooted onto her Jeep's seat and he closed the door. She cranked the engine and looked at him through the open window. "I don't know if you know it yet, but I have a feeling you're going to do really well out here. I actually have toyed with the idea of trying to open up one. I think it's a cool endeavor. Of course, out here it's probably a suitable area just for the summer. It will be interesting to watch and see how you do."

He suspected she would be a superb partner. "I'll see you in a few hours. I'm really glad you came. Drive careful."

She smiled and drove forward.

He watched her leave. This was turning out to be a really great day, and totally not what he had been expecting.

CHAPTER FOUR

Lisa Blair loved being the head chef at the Star Gazer Inn, but she was always happy to have a few hours during the day while her assistant chef took over. Now, she sank into a padded porch chair on the back patio of her recently rented house—the one right beside the inn. Nina had lived here when Alice had bought the inn; then she'd met and married Jackson, Alice's oldest son. That led to Lisa renting the house.

The house enabled Lisa to walk over during her break and relax. It made life so much easier for her because if there were an emergency at the restaurant, she could quickly get over there. If Zane, the chef she had hired to help her out in the busy times, needed her, she could be there immediately. Just like he had told her, he could be there if she needed him. They turned out to be very good working partners. His being her relief gave her rest time that she didn't have the first couple of months when she'd first opened.

Now, when they worked together, they would talk with lots of enjoyment about the food they were cooking. It was very pleasant. She hadn't made a mistake hiring him—he was amazing. Then again, her attraction toward him was highly unexpected, surprising, and unwanted. She wasn't letting anything happen between them—or between her and any man.

Between the history she had with her ex-husband and the divorce itself, she doubted she'd ever get married again. Maybe not even ever date again.

She would just be satisfied with her work and living on this beautiful beach. She was never taking the chance of getting cheated on and then tossed away as if she were worthless.

After she'd divorced him, she'd taken what she'd gotten from her ex-husband and escaped to Europe, trying to forget what she'd been put through. She had taken classes from some of the best chefs, and she had toyed with having an affair with one of them. Instead, knowing it was time to start over, she'd returned to Corpus Christi. Almost immediately, her friend Alice hired her to be the chef of her new inn. It was the perfect opportunity for both of them.

And now, she even had the perfect house next door.

She took a sip of her tea and stared out at the ocean across the beach. Peace rolled over her, thinking about how things were now. After remembering all she'd been through with her ex, she was thoroughly excited to spend the future without him. She had been so blind, but she wasn't anymore. She couldn't even understand how she could have ever loved him. Maybe she felt this way because she wasn't the same person who had married him. And if that were the case, it was a good thing.

Zane returned to the forefront of her thoughts. She immediately shoved the attraction from her mind. That was not happening. She enjoyed cooking with him and knowing that when she wasn't at the inn's kitchen,

Zane was, and she knew she could trust him.

And that was the way it would remain.

* * *

Jackson McIntyre and his beautiful wife, Nina, were just getting back to town after she had gone with him for a meeting with one of the large cattle supply companies. They'd enjoyed a night in town, a meal, and each other's company. But, because she had a lot of painting to work on, getting ready for an art show in Austin, they'd come home. As they reached the ranch's front gate, they saw two small puppies rolling around together on the side of the road.

"Oh goodness! That doesn't look good," Nina said.

"No, it doesn't. Somebody dropped them off." Jackson eased off the gas and slowed down. "I hate to see animals let out like that. So, we'll pick these up, make some calls and try to make sure they aren't lost. If not, we can consider keeping them for the ranch, or for friends for all the other dogs."

"That is what I was hoping you would say."

He had passed them and parked on the side of the road. When they got out of the truck, the puppies raced toward them. "Now stand back so I can greet them first and make sure they will not bite your pretty legs."

"I don't mind if you do, but they don't look mean at all."

They immediately started jumping up and placed their front paws on his legs. Grinning, Jackson bent down and rubbed both of their heads.

"I don't think we have to worry about them attacking." Nina knelt and greeted the pouncing puppies grinning up at her. She laughed, petting both of them. One was black and white with a black circle around each eye, and a white chest and a big black spot across his back. The other one was smaller and a soft sandy color except a white streak that ran between his eyes and down through his nose and then down across his chest. "They are two completely different-looking puppies. I wonder if they were from the same litter, or they have just been dropped off at the same time?"

"I was thinking the same thing."

She rubbed their heads. "I agree. It may be something we never know unless maybe they can do a blood test, although that's not really important. They're both as friendly as the other."

"They react to people the same way."

"They really do. I guess we'll load them up." She grinned at him and picked up the black one she was petting.

Jackson picked up the tan and white puppy, and they strode to the truck and placed them on the backseat's floor. Moments later, he drove through the entrance of the ranch and down the long driveway to the house.

He pulled into the garage and got out. "If we take them inside to bathe them, we'll have to watch them closely in case they need to go outside to go to the bathroom."

She opened the door and helped the puppies out onto the ground. They raced through the garage. "I'll be sure and watch because I won't be keeping them in the house if they're going to do that. Plus, if they're going to be helping you, they'll need to be used to being outside."

"We'll check it all out, but first they need the bath. I'll call around to the vets and see if anybody's reported missing puppies."

They both picked up a puppy before they entered the house and carried them into the kitchen area. They were greeted joyously by Buttercup, who had been dropped off earlier to wait for them. When the cute, curly-haired Goldendoodle noticed the puppy in Nina's arms, it froze.

"Hey, sweetie." She crouched down to introduce Buttercup to the puppies.

"You handle the introductions and I'll get some water for them." He headed to the cabinet to pull out a bowl and fill it with water. He turned and found an enormous smile of delight on Nina's face as she watched her dog rolling on the floor, playing with the pups.

Nina smiled at him, reminding him how much he loved her. "They like each other."

"Yes, they do." He smiled at her and set the water on the ground, and instantly the pups raced to the bowl and started filling up. He looked back at his bride.

Earlier, they had been discussing when they were going to have a baby. Instead of a baby, they suddenly had two extra puppies. That was fine; he liked dogs and she did too, so they were doing okay as long as it didn't interrupt their hope to start their new family.

He had never been as happy as he was since he married Nina in December. And her return to her art career was amazing, but she had been working hard, booking art shows to appear at over the summer. There was a lot to take into consideration during this first year of marriage, and he wanted what was best for her. Maybe having their first baby might need to wait until the second year. Even though they were both ready for a baby, this might not be the right time. They weren't doing anything to prevent her getting pregnant, so he would just have to let the Lord decide these things.

"They get along, so that's great." She stood and moved over to give him a hug.

"Yes, very true. If you've got them for a few moments, I'll go make a few calls and put some notices out. Then we'll bathe them."

She chuckled. "I've got this, and I'll figure out

something to feed them. I guess it will be okay for them to eat some of Buttercup's food."

"Sounds good to me." He headed to his office, smiling as he heard her talking to the animals. He had a feeling she had just found two more animals she could love. She was also very good with the ranch's cow dogs. She was just good…perfect and lovely. And she was going to be a fantastic mother to their baby—or babies—when the time finally arrived.

CHAPTER FIVE

When Sophie returned to the inn, she entered through the side entrance gate and walked around the garden sidewalk. The flowerbed that grew along the area was gorgeous as she moved toward the back porch area. She stopped and studied the beautiful gazebo across the sidewalk on the other side of the house. She assumed it was for events, like small weddings and other celebration events.

Maybe she was getting older and her camping days were easing away, because places like this inn were very inviting. Although, she had made a lot of friends through her camping days and she was still very attracted to that, too.

She went up the steps to the patio. A door led into a hallway right next to the big opening to the living area. If you didn't go in that sliding glass door, the one next to it led into the kitchen, and she could see the cooks and kitchen workers hard at it, cutting up vegetables and working on other food prep. It was between lunch and dinner, so she assumed they were preparing the side dishes for dinner.

Sophie saw a very handsome man she assumed was the chef as he walked around, checking everything being prepared. Another lady walked into the room and she was greeted by everyone. She was beautiful and looked in control as she inspected what the ladies were fixing. She smiled and said something that caused everyone to smile. Then she turned to the male chef, who had been standing quietly watching her; she spoke to him and he followed her into what Sophie assumed was an office. They were both chefs, she believed, and something about the way the man had responded to the woman told her she was the main chef.

Watching the scene hadn't been but for a moment before Sophie headed into the inn. After watching the people in the kitchen, she couldn't wait to eat here. She went up the back stairs and entered her room. At the desk, she wrote a quick email to the camp group. She knew they would love that she was looking for a new place for their first camp of the year and that she would let them know soon. She sent it out, then she got up and headed to the shower.

She was interested in Riley's camp, but she needed to talk about the things that were going to be held there for her campers. Like who was doing the massages and the manicures? And the morning exercise—she usually led that activity, so she just needed to clarify whether that was something they offered or whether she needed to do it. After she got out of her shower and pushed her hair back, she smiled into the mirror because she was glad they were eating dinner together tonight. And then she glanced at her email and was shocked to see all the replies she'd already received back from her camping buddies.

* * *

Riley opened the door to the Star Gazer Inn and walked inside. He was supposed to have been meeting his brother Tucker here for dinner tonight, but instead he was meeting Sophie. Tucker hadn't minded moving their dinner to another night and wished him luck tonight. So here Riley was, about to have dinner with the beautiful Sophie to discuss business. He hoped to get to know her better.

His mom was working the front desk, which she didn't do as often now as she did when they first opened. Now, she was in the office more, but she really enjoyed being at the desk a couple of nights a week to greet her guests. He could have entered through the new private entrance they'd added last month, but he came in the inn's entrance to see his mother. When they had talked earlier in the week, she had said she would be working tonight.

"There you are." She hurried out from behind the counter and threw her arms around him. "I'm so glad to see you. Tucker isn't here yet, but you can get a seat whenever you want to."

"I'm glad to see you too, Mom. Actually, we changed our plans. A woman came out to the camp today and is looking to book a glamping weekend at the end of the month. I'm meeting her here for dinner. She's staying at the inn."

His mom's eyes widened. "Really? Who is it? I must have missed this guest. You know I ask a few questions."

"Sophie Regan. She just checked in this morning before she came out to the camp. I don't think she did more than check in and then look around quickly before heading out."

"I'm excited to get to meet her. It's great you are getting your first booking for your glamping endeavor. I am very pleased for you."

"I am too. And she's a very nice person—a land appraiser. She's appraised land out in this area, but she lives in Corpus, where she has a view of the ocean. But she says it's more of a middle ground for her job, which is spread out throughout the surrounding area of Corpus."

"I can see how that would work."

"Me too. But she really liked it over here, and she has been here to the inn before it closed."

"That's interesting. You'll have to introduce me

when she comes down."

And as if they had produced her from their thoughts, Sophie walked down the stairs in a beautiful sundress that showed off her knees and legs. The soft peach color of her dress complimented her beautiful red hair that swung over her shoulders. She smiled when she saw him. "Hello, Riley. I hope you haven't been waiting long?"

"Not at all. I just walked in. I would like you to meet my mother, the owner of the inn, Alice McIntyre."

"It's really nice to meet you." Alice held her hand out.

"It's really nice to meet you, too. I remember when I came here about six or seven years ago, it was beautiful. However, it is gorgeous now. Amazing."

"Thank you. I actually used to work here in the summers before I met my son's dad. After we got married, we would come visit for a weekend or two each year. It was a special place for me. I was so sad and lost after he died that I would come out here and walk on the beach. And one day I decided to buy it. It helped me move my life forward, and I love everything about it. I have so many memories here, and I hated seeing it closed. Now we get to help others have memories, and I'm so glad you're here. If you need anything and I'm not working at the desk, I live farther down there, past the stairs. Just knock on the door anytime."

"Thank you. That's kind. I'm sure I'll be fine, though. I think you're a very smart woman, buying this inn. I'm also so sorry that you lost your husband." She looked from her to Riley. "And that you lost your father. I actually understand, because I lost my mom and dad years ago."

"Thank you, and I'm sorry for you too," Riley said. "It's hard getting used to, but we've learned to be honored by the time we had with him. I hope you feel the same."

"I agree with Riley," Alice said. "We are so sorry for your loss."

"Thank you both. My parents died in a car wreck when I was young, and my grandmother finished raising me. I was blessed to have her, but she died several years ago."

"It seems you have a great outlook on life, and that is wonderful. The way I look at it is we were blessed to have our loved ones for a time. And I'm sure they are glad you do things, like camping, to make your life special. Riley's new venture is going to be great. He's loving every moment of getting it ready, and he's especially looking forward to glamping. You'll be Riley's first glamping trip and I'm sure he'll do a wonderful job for you. Now, your table is probably ready, so you two should go on in."

"Thank you, Mom, for the great review."

Sophie hugged his mom. "It was really nice meeting you. I will see you again before I leave."

Alice smiled as they hugged. "I agree. Now, enjoy yourselves."

After his mom walked away they walked beside each other to the door that took them into the waiting area of the restaurant.

He looked at Sophie. "You made my mom's day. She thought I was having dinner with my brother tonight. When I told her we had changed our plans and

I was having a business meeting with one of her guests, she was shocked. When I told her it was a delightful woman checking out a glamping trip, she got excited. I hate to tell you this, but I believe she was mostly happy because I was meeting a woman. It's been a long time since I went on a date, and though I told her this was business, not a date, she was still thrilled."

"I'm sure mothers are excited to see their son around a lady when they haven't gone out in a long time. Even though this is a business date, it gives her hope, I guess."

"Exactly." He smiled, then they followed the hostess to their table on the patio, which was what he had requested when he called in the reservation.

The table was next to the railing. He pulled Sophie's chair out for her, then pushed it in closer to the table after she sat down.

"Thank you." She smiled up at him.

"You're welcome." He smiled back and took the chair across from her. "Now, you know I'm paying for this because you're here to do business with me, so no arguments."

"Fine, but I didn't mean for you to do that."

"I imagine not, but I am totally excited about you and your group. You're the one who sparked my interest in this when we met at the gas station, so it's great to hope that you're going to be my first glamping group."

Her expression softened in delight. "It is cool. I sent a quick email earlier to all the registered campers to ask them if they would like to come here or not. I wasn't expecting to have so many answers by now, but after I got out of the shower and got dressed, I checked my email, and it was crazy how many had already replied back that they were excited and still attending. They love the idea of being here, and to be the first glamping event for your camp made them thrilled to be the part of that. Plus, the location is great for most of our members. So, just to let you know, unless your price is horrible, then it's going to happen, and we haven't even discussed everything."

He was startled and pleased by her reply. "It's

awesome to know my inspiration is the first to book a glamping weekend. Whether I have more after that we'll see, but I just have a good feeling that if I can do well by all your members that it's going to be a great beginning."

She smiled again, something he was getting very used to seeing. "That's great. I'm glad to be involved that way."

The waitress returned with their tea and said she'd return for their orders in a few minutes. After she left, Sophie looked out over the landscape of the inn and out to the ocean.

"It's beautiful, isn't it?" Riley glanced at the view, then back at her. She was beautiful.

"Very. Once I realized this had reopened, I was determined I was going to come back for a visit. The minute I had the cancelation of the previous camp, I knew I was coming here. I wasn't really even horribly disappointed because I was looking so forward to visiting the inn while checking out the new camping spot. Then finding that it was you who owns the new camp, and that the inn's owner is your mother…it's just really wonderful."

"I feel very similar. I think it's great."

"I'm excited about both, and I'm sure my ladies are going to love the camp too. Will you be working that weekend so they'll get to meet you?"

"I wouldn't miss my glamping grand opening for anything. Tonight, we'll discuss everything you want, what I have planned, and if it's agreeable to you. And since this will be my first one, I would appreciate any suggestions that y'all have enjoyed other places that could improve what I have planned. I went to one. It looked like everyone was enjoying themselves, and that's what I want to give you ladies."

"I'll try to help however I can. This is the first one of the year, and we're always excited to see each other after a few winter months off."

"So, with the change of location, do you think from the reactions you've seen so far that the original number of fifty-five might still come?"

"I don't know yet, but the response on that email so far is looking good. Most ladies love our beach trips so if they can make the extra miles they'll come."

"You don't always book at a beach?"

"No, but at least three trips are to the beach. The other times are nice lakes situated deeper in the state and closer to some of the members. I've always tried to keep the same destinations if we've really enjoyed them. But sometimes the dates are not available and we try out new places, like here. And believe me, your destination is perfect and beautiful, and they loved the pictures. I think it's going to be awesome."

He hoped so, because he really liked her. "You have a very positive attitude, and I agree with you—I think the temperature is going to be great, mostly. The water could still be a little too cold for some, but as you saw today, it's very pleasant out there. And when we get the tents up and the lights going and the musicians playing music at night, it will be great for all you ladies to enjoy visiting."

"Sounds perfect."

The waitress returned for their orders.

Riley gave her a smile. "Sorry, we've been talking, so give us a few more minutes, please."

"Certainly." The waitress smiled and left them.

"I guess we better pause our talk and pick out something to eat." Every extra minute the meal took was okay with him.

"Sounds good. I am kind of hungry. I've only eaten breakfast this morning."

"Eat anything you want—it's all great. Believe me, the main chef here is amazing. Her name is Lisa. Do you know that her assistant chef used to be the head chef at Grandberry's in Corpus Christi?"

"Zane Tyson is a great cook, and from what I've heard Lisa is too, so this should be amazing."

"I agree, so let's test them out."

Moments later, after the waitress left with their orders, Riley had to remind himself this was business, not personal. The last thing he wanted to do was get carried away and run off her and her group because he couldn't keep his mind focused on business.

Pulling out the paper he had folded in his shirt pocket, he laid it on the table in front of her. "Here's the cost sheet that I've brought for you to study. Tell me honestly what you think about it and we'll discuss it. If there is something you don't agree with, then we'll come up with whatever works for you. If it's less money than I think I can manage, we'll work down to where I can host it for you and at least have a learning experience for me."

"Okay." Her eyes widened as she looked at the page. "Are you sure this is all? It's very reasonable, but you might figure out after we do this that you need to raise your prices. It's going to be outstanding, I think."

"Maybe so, but we'll go with it and I'll learn from this. I'm hoping that after the weekend is over, you'll think the camp is as good as you're thinking it is right now."

"I am very willing to help you make sure of it, so if there's anything you need to know, I'll be here tomorrow. And after I leave, you can contact me by phone or email."

"I'm going to tell you right now that that's an amazing offer, and I'm going to take you up on it."

Riley was enthused by her offer and was fairly certain she had no idea how much.

CHAPTER SIX

Lisa spotted Alice out on the porch and moved to visit with her. They had been in this inn together since the beginning, and though she didn't actually own any of it, she had an investment in the kitchen's profit.

"Hey," she greeted Alice as she turned to see what her friend was looking at and spotted it immediately. "Who is that lady with Riley? He looks very interested." Indeed he did.

Alice gave her a delighted grin. "Her name is Sophie Regan, and she is here looking into a group of ladies renting his campground."

"He looks very pleased," Lisa said. All of Alice's

sons were wonderful, and she enjoyed them all. However, Riley hadn't been here in a couple of months. "I'm going to go by and say hello and give them a free dessert."

"You know he's going to refuse that since all my boys refuse free meals from here. They want to pay and support us when they come eat your wonderful meals."

"I know. They tell me if I don't charge them that I'm making you mad because I'll be sending them to another restaurant."

Alice grinned. "They are taking care of the two of us. So how are you going to talk him into a piece of pie?"

"I'll make him feel like he needs to. You'll see." Lisa chuckled, knowing it was all true. Alice's sons adamantly believed in helping the business do well. She knew every one of them could easily afford to pay the cost, but so could Alice, considering their ranch was worth so much. "I better speak to them and some of the others before I go back and make sure that Zane has the kitchen under control."

Alice placed her hand on Lisa's arm. "You and Zane still getting along well?"

She did not miss the twinkle in her friend's eyes. "We are getting along wonderfully. He is an amazing chef. When we're thinking about improvements or fine-tuning the menu, he will give me an idea, but he always goes with my ideas because he says it's my restaurant and it should reflect my concepts."

"I agree," Alice said.

"But Zane is an amazing chef. I don't mind if he has an idea that makes it better, but he always goes for my plan. No matter what."

"And it's obvious that bothers you. But you are a wonderful chef. We all know that the restaurant was already doing wonderful before he hired on. That's why you had to hire him. Therefore, it's not like he's lying to you—he just believes in you, obviously."

Lisa sighed. It could be true, but she felt in her heart that he wasn't completely telling the truth. "Maybe so. Anyway, I'm going to talk to Riley and his date and then go back to the kitchen. Not that I'm worried about it…I just like to let my presence be known in the dining room and the kitchen."

"I hear you. Enjoy. I'm heading back inside." Alice smiled and left while Lisa entered the small gate into the patio area.

"Lisa, it's good to see you," Riley greeted her as she headed their way. He stood and hugged her.

"So good to see you here, Riley." She patted his arm as he released her, and she looked at his guest.

"I'd like to introduce you to Sophie Regan."

"No, don't stand." Lisa shook the pretty woman's hand. "It's really nice to meet you. I was talking to Alice, and she said you were going to bring your camping group to use Riley's new campground. That's wonderful."

"I am so excited to have a new place for my group. I came early to enjoy this fabulous inn and restaurant. I love it, so you may see me more often because when I travel by myself, I don't take my little camper with me. And I do like to get out of town on the weekends."

Lisa felt that that was not said just for her benefit when she saw Riley's expression. She had a feeling he was really interested in Sophie.

"I think that's a great idea," he said, the pleased look on his face growing.

It was time for her to let them have dinner alone. "I just wanted to stop by and say I'm glad to meet you. I know you'll enjoy camping out there. I'm going to send out a couple of free pieces of pie for you two to celebrate the agreement. It's my treat." She looked at Riley and lifted a warning eyebrow.

"I am not going to turn down a paid-for piece of pie, since you are obviously determined from that warning expression. I'd rather pay for it, but I'll take your pies any way I can get them."

"Perfect. Tonight, we have banana cream pie and coconut cream pie. I thought I would send you one of each or, if you have a preference, let me know. We also have several other desserts if you'd rather have something else."

He looked at Sophie and hitched a brow. "I'm good for one of each. We can share and you can get a taste for both. Or if you want something different, just let this lovely lady know."

Sophie looked at Lisa. "I'm with Riley. I would love to taste both of them."

"Perfect choice. So nice to meet you. Have a great dinner." Lisa headed toward the kitchen. She wondered whether Alice had noticed the interest in Riley's eyes when he looked at this beautiful camper.

* * *

The following morning, Riley picked Sophie up after breakfast and he took her to meet the massage therapist and the two manicurists who would be there that weekend her group came to camp. All three ladies worked at the same spa on Star Gazer Island. They would fit in with the group well. She liked that her campers would get what they'd come for and paid for. They exercised first thing in the morning with her and then enjoyed the relaxing massage and manicure.

When they got outside, she looked at Riley. "You did so good. Unless they are terrible at their jobs, they'll be a success with the ladies."

He smiled warmly. "I'm glad you think that way,

because that's what I'm hoping. The masseuse will have several soaking tubs full of warm water, oils, and all kinds of good stuff. Do you think your ladies will enjoy that?"

"We've had that before, not every time, but it's very popular."

"Great." They had reached his truck. He held her door open before he went around and climbed inside and looked over at her. "Since I'm from a large ranch not too far out from here, I had an idea. I've been thinking that I can bring some horses to camp and we can do some beach rides. We do a few groups Saturday morning, Saturday afternoon, and Sunday morning before everyone heads home that afternoon. What do you think?"

She gaped at him. "I love it. I think that would be a huge hit."

"Awesome. Everyone will be arriving through Friday afternoon, and we can have signup time then, or they can go over to the horse area and sign up later. That might be best, but either way works."

"Whatever you think."

"Perfect. Since you like the idea of horses, I thought I'd drive out to the ranch with you and let you meet the horses and make sure you think they are tame enough. I have horses that are very tame, and the ladies could ride them safely, but there are some that have a little more energy. Do you ride?"

"Yes, I love to ride, and I'm fairly sure a lot of women in our group can. And also, those who don't might want to try if the horse was calm enough. Whatever you think—you're the leader."

She enjoyed watching a smile spread across his handsome face. The man really wanted to do whatever worked for her group. She appreciated that.

"I think everyone will enjoy it. Let's head out there and check out the horses."

* * *

Riley enjoyed the ride to the ranch, talking with Sophie. She had been doing these camping trips for several years, it seemed, and had fun stories to share.

They finally pulled into the drive of the family

ranch. He lived in a cabin, letting Jackson and his wife, Nina, live in the main house. Jackson and Tucker ran the ranch, which was fine with him because he enjoyed working on the ranch and helping however they needed him. But they knew he had been distracted, eager to try something new. The camp had fascinated him and when he'd told them, they had been supportive.

He looked over at her. "So, you have been doing this awhile—does it ever get in the way of dating?"

Sophie cringed. "I actually got tired of dating. I guess I'm hard to please. I'm just determined that when I get married, it will be the right person. Five years ago, I was practically dating someone new every weekend. I was not feeling anything to hold me to any of them. And dating all the time was keeping me from enjoying things I really wanted…things like camping, because I was dining out with men and looking for my future. Someone I wanted to spend the rest of my life with. It just wasn't happening.

"I decided to quit focusing my weekends on dating, and I agreed to go on a camping trip with one of my girlfriends. We went to a lake with a group of her friends and stayed in her camper. We went fishing and had a great weekend. Her friends were awesome, but as I was sitting there that evening having dinner with the group, I had this idea about adding a little more pampering. Massages and manicures—and now this horse riding is a great idea, I have to tell you—but anyway, I sat there and talked to them and before I left that weekend, several of them told me to please let them know if I actually developed my camping group. By the end of the next two months, I had sent out an email to everyone who asked to come along, and my group started. And as strange as it sounds, I haven't dated in the last five years. I just grew weary of trying to meet the right man and I hadn't felt drawn to anybody. And if I'm not, then there is no reason to go out."

She was absolutely right. He had felt the same way. "I know that feeling. I used to date a good bit but stopped and focused on this camp and didn't even miss dating. Anyway, speaking of camping, let's go meet my brother and his wife—"

"The one who painted the bathroom's painting?"

"Yes, Nina is a talented lady and was living next door to the inn when Mom bought it. Jackson and Nina are a great couple. Nina had been hiding from a scammer who had threatened her, stolen from her and was hunting her after she hid here in Star Gazer. When Jackson learned her story, he helped find the jerk, kept her safe, and fell in love with her. It's a romantic story."

"Very. And scary. I'm glad he was able to help her."

"Me too. You'll like her. They are home today and Tucker is too, I think. Jackson runs the business part of the ranch and Tucker runs the ranch part with the horses and the cattle. I mentioned the horse rides to him, and he thought it was a really cool idea. He'll be glad to make sure the amount of horses we need will be ready. Also, a couple of our guys will be there to lead the show, so it's not something I have to worry about. And Tucker will be at the camp too, taking stress off me. I need to make sure everything else is going smoothly for all of you."

She pointed her beautiful smile at him. "I can't wait to meet everybody—your sister-in-law, your brothers and the horses."

They got out of the truck just as Nina came out of the house's side door with a big smile on her face. Jackson strode behind her.

"Nina and Jackson, this is Sophie."

"I am so glad you came out to see the horses." Nina shook Sophie's hand. "And I am really glad that you are going to fulfill Riley's desire to have this glamping portion of his new camp. A lot of women are going to be happy with this special camping trip. We're thrilled that you might decide to put horse riding on the list of things to do."

She smiled and looked at him. "I'm excited about Riley's suggestion. The idea of the ladies riding horses is great. I couldn't wait to get to your ranch to check them out. I'm also glad to meet both of you. I saw the painting you put in the restroom and loved it. I've heard your story of what you were put through and how you became a part of their family." She looked from a smiling Nina to Jackson.

Jackson pulled Nina back against his chest and kissed her cheek. "I'm sorry she went through her ordeal but I am grateful we met. We ended up a perfect fit. Even though I wish her life had been better before moving here."

"We do, too," Riley said. "But life is what brings people to their loves. You two are a perfect example of that."

"Yes, it sounds that way," Sophie agreed.

"You're right—we are." Nina smiled up at Jackson.

Sophie saw their love expressions and her heart squeezed. She looked away before her longing was seen by anyone else. She noticed a large tent set up between the house and the barns and then looked at Riley.

"That's where the dinner tonight is taking place. There's something like fifty buyers coming."

"That's right," Nina said. "And, Sophie, you're invited too, if you're going to still be here."

Jackson agreed. "We'd be glad to have you, if you don't mind being in the middle of a bunch of cattle people."

"Thank you. I really appreciate your invitation, but I'll be heading home tonight."

"Well, if you change your mind, I'm sure that Riley will fix you up. Probably pick you up, bring you out and take you back to the inn."

"Yes, I would." Riley winked at her.

"Thanks. It's tempting, but I have work to do tomorrow preparing for the appraisal I do on Monday plus a few other things."

"Okay, we'll let you go see the horses. I hope to see you again." Nina grinned, then turned and headed back to the house. Jackson waved and joined his wife.

"Bye and thank you," she called, then fell into step with Riley walking toward the barn.

Riley looked at her and smiled as he led the way down the center walkway, through the barn, and out into the back arena area.

"Tucker and his men gathered these up for us. Tucker said these are the horses that we could count on for their ability to be ridden by everyone. Even those who don't have a lot of experience."

"This is a great idea. I haven't been to any beach

camp yet that offered this. I'm sure that there are some that do it, but not where we've gone. Anyway, I'm excited about the thought."

"Would you like to ride now?"

"You've got a busy day. I mean, I don't want to take up your time when you've got a dinner to go to tonight and I need to head on back this evening."

"All I have to do is change my outfit and if we get really sweaty on the horses, I guess take a shower. But it's not going to be a hard thing considering I have to take you back to the inn anyway. If I'm late, it's not a big deal. Tucker is going to be there and is probably going to ride up any minute."

Everything he said was tempting her. If taking a ride on the horse meant spending more time with him before she left, then that was good. However, she wasn't staying around for the party because she had the appraisal to get ready for just as she'd told him. But the horse ride as too tempting.

"Come on—just a short ride."

"Very well. I would love to go for a short ride.

And then I'll anticipate the ride during camp."

"Awesome. Let's go get a couple of horses."

Within moments, they had the two horses saddled and were riding out to the pasture. Feeling full of excitement, Sophie looked over at Riley. He looked so handsome and absolutely relaxed and natural in his saddle. "It's been a good while since I rode, but I still love it and you look like you do too."

"I do." He hitched a brow. "I've ridden all my life. It's almost as if I was born on a horse."

They rode across some beautiful land and down to a large lake. It would have been a great place for her camping group's camp. But that would put a lot of people tromping on his land, bothering his cattle as they strolled around all over the place, and she knew that wasn't good.

"You and your family have an absolutely amazing place."

"Thank you. My dad and my grandfather created it, and then we've been brought up here, loving it. My dad died in an accident crossing the river as we were herding cattle, so since then, it's mostly been us overseeing everything. Tucker and Jackson were already in charge of their areas back then because Dad was training them, so they could take over."

"You didn't take any major position?"

He slowed at the bank of the lake and then stopped and gazed out over the water. "No. I love the ranch, but I'd been restless before Dad died. Dad wasn't forcing any of us to stay at the ranch. Dallas chose bull riding competitions, and I just wasn't sure what I wanted. After Dad died, my brothers knew I enjoyed going and picking up horses or cattle and not being stuck on the ranch, so I picked them up or delivered them to buyers. That's what I had been doing when I met you at that gas station. I was coming back from having delivered a trailer of cattle. You were interesting, and after talking to you I latched on to finding out more about this type of camping." He smiled at her.

"That's great."

He held her gaze, causing tingles throughout her.

"You inspired me, and I went to researching it and knew almost instantly that I wanted to open one. It's not like I have to keep it going for the rest of my life. I can keep it running by hiring someone, or if I get into it and I don't like it, then I can close it down. But—"

"If you like it, you can keep it going." She smiled at him and he nodded with a smile. She reached over and placed her hand over his briefly. "I think you're going to like it. And just think about all the people you're going to get to know. The women, I mean, who you'll get to know. Maybe you'll find a wife among them."

"I don't know. But you and me both might meet somebody who interests us. Like right now."

Her breath caught. "I should not have said anything about you finding a wife. Sorry. Anyway, I really enjoy riding the horses, but I'd better get back to my vehicle and head home."

"You didn't bother me with your statement. But you're right—it's time to get you on the road toward home."

CHAPTER SEVEN

She enjoyed seeing the ranch and meeting Riley's family. They seemed very nice, and it was tempting to stay another night and go to the party they were throwing. Not because she was interested in the party—rather, she was interested in spending more time with Riley. And this bothered her.

She hadn't dated anyone in so long. Why would she feel this attraction to him? She had finally settled into being single, but she could admit there were times she wished that someone was out there meant for her. She had just been convinced there wasn't, and that's why she had started living her life, not focused on looking for love.

She had given up building her life around meeting the man of her future. But this Riley was the first man she had met during the last several years who even made her think about not being single. The first man who made her think about the future. And she hadn't missed that he was attracted to her. It wasn't something new, because she had seen that look several times from men. However, she felt absolutely nothing for them and had never been tempted until now.

As they got back into the barn area, a tall, handsome man with a similarity to Riley walked toward them, smiling.

"Tucker, I thought you'd show up," Riley greeted him.

"I didn't get here as soon as I thought I would. I was busy checking out some cattle, but I'm glad I made it." He had both hands on his hips and smiled at her. "I'm Tucker McIntyre, Riley's brother. Did you enjoy your ride?"

"It's great to meet you. And yes, it was beautiful. I really think the ladies are going to love being able to have such magnificent horses to ride along the beach. I know I am."

Tucker's lips curved in a smile. "That's great. My brother has been working hard on this, and you were the inspiration. So when he called and told me you had agreed on the horses, I was glad, but knew he was happier than me."

She saw the look on Riley's face saying he wished he could make his brother quit talking. That just made her insides quiver a bit. He dismounted and so she did, too, before either man could come over and help her.

"I believe we're going to use all twenty." Riley grinned at her as he let the stuff his brother said slip away. "She's going to book that last weekend of April. And she's willing to give me any advice she has from all the different places she's visited. I think it's going to be the best way to open up my camp, with some expert advice."

His words thrilled her—made her feel needed, and she loved that.

His brother looked just as thrilled by his words. "I think that's great for both of you. If you get there and it's not like you want, you just tell him what you need and he'll get it done, I can promise you. Or he'll call over here to the ranch to me and tell me to get out there to get it fixed." He laughed. "I'm just teasing. This man is a man who can get things done. I've been working with him a little bit, just because I needed a change too. Getting the buildings and camping spots together was a fun endeavor. Who knows, I may be the next one opening a camp somewhere."

She laughed, liking him. "You did a great job."

"We're going to head out. She needs to get back and I do too. Would you mind unsaddling these?"

Tucker took the reins. "I don't mind at all. Y'all get back because I know you've got to get dressed for this evening. Jackson told me he was going to see if you wanted to stay. Are you going to?"

"No, I have to get back. And there's nothing for me to do there except bug y'all and eat." She grinned. "I've got an appraisal on Monday and I need to prepare for it plus emails to the ladies who will attend the first glamping camp here."

Riley grinned at her. "Which I think is perfect since you're the one who inspired me to do this camp. You're the absolute perfect person to be the first event."

"I'm thrilled about that," she said. "It was nice to meet you, Tucker."

"Same here. And I'll help Riley out at the camp if he needs it, especially with the horses."

"Perfect."

A few minutes later, Riley pulled the truck onto the road and he looked at her. "Tucker had a blast the few times he's been able to help me get the camp ready. That's really good for him."

"Why is it good for him?"

"He was in the Marines, and he fell for a nurse at the camp where he was stationed. Then she was killed by an explosive, and he was never the same afterward. It was right near his release, so he came home different from the guy he'd been before he joined the Marines. We've given him space and let him work hard on the ranch and deal with it as needed. So not only did he lose Dad, but he also lost the woman he loved. It's been rough on him."

"I'm so sorry he's gone through that. Like y'all, I've lost my parents, and it's terribly tough to get over. But to lose the love of your life and a parent at the same time has to be horrible."

"Tucker is a strong guy. I'm hoping he will fall in love again one day and make a complete healing, but right now I'm just excited to see his interest in something other than cows. He perks up when he comes out to the camp."

"Wonderful. I'm glad he's finding his way."

"Me too. I think working at the camp will help him."

"I do too." She hated what his brother had gone through, and was glad that he had understanding, supportive brothers.

He looked over at her. His eyes locked with hers, sending a warm shiver through her.

"You know, I open this next weekend, if you get the craving to come down to test it out. Get the feel of the place."

It was tempting. "I'll let you know. I have a few ranches on the other side of Corpus, and I have to get them looked at and then the report written up. I just don't know if I'll have the time. But we'll see."

He had pulled into town, turned the corner and

headed toward the inn. "I totally understand. I just wanted to make sure you knew you were welcome. And no charge, if you come."

She smiled at him as he pulled into the drive. "Thank you for such a gracious invitation. And such an enjoyable weekend. My vehicle is already packed, so just pull there beside it. I moved out this morning so they could get it ready for whoever else needed it tonight. I've told your mom and Lisa that the stay was wonderful and the food fantastic and I will be back."

"Great." He smiled as he walked with her to her Jeep.

Their arms brushed, and a tingle ran through her. She hadn't felt an attraction for a guy in a long time, and she was honestly uncertain about her reaction. Heart pounding, she pushed the unlock button and it unlocked. Riley reached for the handle the same time she did, and their hands met on the door handle.

"I'll get it," he said softly.

She took a breath and pulled her hand back, though it was really hard.

"Thank you," she said quietly as he opened the

door. She started to slide into her seat, but to her surprise, he slid his arm around her and hugged her. Shivers of delight rushed through every part of her.

"Thank you for coming. It really means a lot to me." He let her go and held her gaze.

She couldn't look away from him. "I'm just as thrilled about coming to the camp as you are about having your first one. So I think we are a good couple—I mean, camp partners."

"I agree with you. Drive safe, okay?" He stepped back as she slid onto her car seat. Then he winked at her, closed the door and stepped farther back.

Her hand shook as she put the key into the ignition. She met his gaze through the windshield as she backed out. Sophie pulled out onto the road. When she looked into her rearview mirror, he still stood there.

She had never been this thrilled in her life.

* * *

"Meeting Sophie today was interesting," Tucker said at

the party that evening. "I mean, I was shocked when you told me she had arrived here and was interested in the camp. But she's beautiful *and* interested in you."

"She is beautiful, and I agree she's interested in the camp, but I think in me too. But there's something holding her back. She hasn't dated in about five years. She just got tired of putting her dating as priority and then nothing coming of it while everything else she was interested in passed her by, like camping. So she went out on a camping trip with a friend and then started her own camping group, and it's very successful. She's put dating on the back burner and seems very happy. So I don't know if me getting interested in her would be a good idea."

"You're already interested."

"Okay, yes, I'm already interested. But believing this thought in my head that she's interested in me might be a bad thing."

"It's a good thing. You haven't really found anybody who you're interested in, and you haven't dated in a while. Don't pass up seeing what happens, or you'll regret it for the rest of your life."

Riley knew his brother was thinking about the loss of his love. "What about you, Tucker? After losing your love, you started back dating, but it's obvious you don't date long. But you seem happier when you're dating. Are you searching for a new love?"

"I've tried dating, but so far, no feeling other than friendship. I haven't gone out lately, since watching Jackson and Dallas both fall in love with wonderful ladies. I just know that when I'm taking somebody out, it reminds me of what I can't do with Darla since she was killed."

Riley knew all of this; Darla's death right before his brother completed his enlistment tore Tucker up. "I'm so sorry you had to go through such a loss."

"Me too. But I know from losing Darla how important love is. I've gotten to watch our brothers fall in love and now, you could. I'm rooting for you and will help you with the camp any way I can. She's really nice. To be honest, lately I've been concentrating on work and then helping you when you need me. Weirdly, it helps me get further along down the line."

Riley was so sorry for what his brother went through, and he hoped one day he would find someone who could fill the holes left by his obviously wonderful love. "You're encouraging me to go for it? Even though you're about to shut down any attempt to find love again?"

"I'm doing what I need to do in order to move on and it's not dating. It's working on the ranch, keeping busy. I find it interesting that you met Sophie at a gas station, and you were immediately interested, not just in her but in this camping idea. Then, before you even opened, she shows up and books your first glamping camp. I wouldn't let those coincidences go without making sure you check it out thoroughly. For you, I think this interest in Sophie is more like my relationship with Darla. See where it goes."

Riley had to agree with his brother. And now he just had to figure out how to do it right.

* * *

The day after the ranch dinner and sale, Nina was tired.

She'd helped plan the dinner while they were on his business trip. Then they'd gotten home and found the adorable puppies, who were still with them after a week. She'd attended the dinner but had not made it through the sale. She'd come inside, gotten the pups and taken them outside to go potty. They'd done that quickly, and then she'd sank down on the patio chair and watched them roll together in the grass. They were adorable and made her think of two toddlers playing— and that made her heart yearn even more for a baby of her own.

She and Jackson had discussed beginning their family, and so they had begun trying as soon as she'd gotten off her birth control medicine. But so far, in over the three months that they'd been attempting, no baby had been created. Now, as Nina sat in the chair with the puppies playing with her sweet Buttercup, her heart pounded with wanting. She had nothing she knew of that would keep her from having a baby, no symptoms of anything that would stop her from getting pregnant. She knew many women took longer trying for a baby, so she needed to just quit worrying.

She needed to enjoy Buttercup and these two darling puppies they had picked up from the side of the road. They'd quickly attached themselves to her, Jackson, and Buttercup, and they'd become attached to them. In the three days she had been in her art studio—which was what used to be the flower room of the house—the puppies had played on the floor, slept in all kinds of areas, and then taken her outside to play. She had enjoyed every moment they had been around her. She had even added a couple of puppies to the painting she was working on of a countryside and a lake.

Now, here in the dark, watching them play, her thoughts whirled.

She gathered the dogs into the house and put the puppies into the laundry room; then she went upstairs. After getting ready for bed, she left the light on in the bathroom for Jackson. She crawled into bed and passed out, dreaming of the baby she was so ready to hold and love.

CHAPTER EIGHT

Riley and his small crew made sure that they knew how they were going to handle the weekend of campers. The small kitchen/concession stand group made lunch for everybody, and they practiced getting their stuff done. The grounds guy, who was also the trash man, was a retired man from the area who loved being outside and had applied for the job because it would give him something to do. The cleaning lady took care of the bathrooms and helped keep the towels handed out to anybody who needed one for the beach or the showers. It was a small group, but it was a good group.

Later he might need more help, but this was plenty

for this first regular camping group. When he did the glamping weekends, it would be more complicated with catered dinners; lunch and breakfast would be provided by his crew at the food bar. He had other things to take care of too; he just had to get it all figured out before he had a glamping camp.

He was standing at the gate when the campers started arriving. He gave them each a number to where they would put their tent or camper. He noticed a lot of families with several excited kids. He enjoyed being able to give them a nice place to hit the beach like he and his brothers had done with his mom and dad.

People were already in the ocean, and kids were running around, smiling. Several people told him how beautiful everything was and how glad they had gotten to come to the private beach camping. He liked to see all the smiles on everybody's faces.

He loved helping families enjoy time together over the weekend. And even though he had opened a place because he had met Sophie and wanted to hold group gatherings, he knew he enjoyed doing this for families too. He was glad he had done at least two weeks for families and then one or two weeks for groups.

As he stood there, watching everyone at the food area eating and looking happy, he heard an engine and turned to see who was arriving. A smile burst across his face.

Sophie waved out the window of the Jeep. "Hi, I decided to join your first week," she called from where she had stopped next to the office.

"Great to see you," he said, reaching her quickly. "And happy you decided to come check us out."

"Me too. It was kind of sudden since I was able to get my work done for the week. So I loaded up my little camper and came to test it out."

"Well, I'm very glad you're here. Now let's go find you a place to park that cute little camper." He gave her a number that was on the end and close to his, which was back behind the small office.

She had backed her tiny camper in as if it were something she did every day, and he unhooked it from her Jeep. She parked her Jeep beside the camper and came to stand beside him. She'd connect her camper to the water and drain hookups later.

"So what do you think about this area now that you're seeing people parking here and you have your own spot?"

"I think it looks great. And from what I see, they all must have gotten here earlier today and are enjoying themselves. They love this place."

Relief washed over him. "That's kind of what I'm feeling, too, and it really is pleasing."

"I'm sure it is. And you just wait—at the end of the month, when all of my ladies show up, they're going to love it too."

He stared at her and couldn't help thinking how beautiful she was, how encouraging and excited she was for her ladies who were coming. "I think if they're in the least bit like you, then what you say will be true. At least I hope so."

Her smile widened. "Wonderful. I'll take that as a compliment."

"It definitely was."

"Great. Now, I have to get something to eat. I was hungry when I got off work, but I said, 'No you don't;

you are not going to eat until you get there at the camp and try one of their meals.'"

"Then say no more. I haven't eaten supper either. Though it's the same as the lunch menu so let's go test them out."

"That's what I was hoping you would say."

"Great. Let's go fill our hungry stomachs and then take a walk on the beach, if you want to. Or you can do whatever you want to—this is your weekend."

"Let's go with your plan." She smiled at him and sent his insides rolling.

They walked across the sand and took one of the tables surrounding the cafe. Menus were against the napkin holder; they each took one and in a quick moment, a young college-age waitress came to ask for their order.

Sophie smiled up at her. "I think I'm going to try this Texas fajita wrap. It sounds great. With french fries, please. And then I'm going to try your unsweet tea."

"Mandy, make me the same and we'll both test it out."

"Sure thing. I'll be right back with your tea." Mandy smiled and headed off.

"Everybody eating here looks happy. You can tell—look at that family over there with the two young kids in their swimming suits and the grinning daddy and mom have had a wonderful day."

"They really have. I saw them play in the water, and they made sandcastles, as did the other families. All the families and friends have been enjoying themselves all day. It makes me extremely happy. Nobody has complained. You know, I'm doing this in part so people can tell me if there's something wrong. I'm hoping by the time your group arrives, if there's something wrong, I'll have it fixed."

"I'm confident you can handle anything. But that's why I came, to help you figure things out if you need to, just like we talked about."

He didn't tell her that mostly what he had been talking about was just getting to see her again, but he would use whatever it took to make that happen. "I'm thankful for that, and I'm very glad you're here."

* * *

Later that evening, after they had eaten, they walked a little on the beach. Sophie had completely loved every moment. She looked at him and smiled. "I'm very glad I came today."

"I am too."

"How did the event last weekend go?"

"Very well. My sister-in-law and brother were happy that it turned out well, but they wished you had gotten to be there."

"I wish I could have come too. However, getting back home and getting all my work done enabled me to come to camp tonight."

"And I'm really glad about that. And when they learn you came to camp tonight, they'll be happy."

"Your family seems proud that you're doing this."

"They are."

They walked in silence for a few steps.

"So what do you think about your people who are coming? Is it going to be most of them or half of them?"

Sophie was enjoying the evening and so glad she'd come. "There's going to be about forty-five. The change of timing and the distance was part of that, but the rest of them are excited to try a new place out. Especially since you saved the day. You should get a good bit of excellent information from this group."

"That is great. Did they tell you anything in particular they were excited to have?"

The wind blew strands of red hair into her face, and she pushed it away and smiled. "No. They were just thrilled to come and see your camp and meet you. They know that part of why you opened the camp was because you heard about them. They're thrilled about that—just like I am."

He smiled, and it made her smile bigger. He was so handsome, and she liked his expressions, even without a smile. Goodness, she was just unnerved at how he made her feel. It had been so long since she had been attracted to anyone; was it something she wanted to test out once again?

He stopped walking and stared out at the waves for a minute, then at her. "I have to tell you, I'm happy you came this weekend. But my gladness has nothing to do with the camp at the end of the month. To be honest, I'm very attracted to you."

She took a breath, trying to calm her shaking nerves. "I'm glad to see you, too, and yes, I am attracted to you. It's been years since I was attracted to anyone and it's thrown me off-balance a bit."

His smile widened and his eyes twinkled. "It makes me a little nervous, too. With the camp and this new attraction to you, I don't want to do anything to upset you."

She looked away and out to sea, trying to get her thoughts right. "We're going to take this a little at a time. My priority is my group's camping trip, and our attraction comes next."

"No worries. I'll put my business face on and host your party just like I had planned and not let my interest in you mess anything up."

He was a great man and was attracted to her. Their camping deal at the end of the month made their situation difficult. And they were both determined to make that right. "All right, so what does that mean for us now?"

"It means we'll figure it out. The sun is setting, and I need to roam the camp a little bit, make sure everyone is happy and all my workers at the food bar are doing okay. That reminds me to tell you that now it's open until ten o'clock but at your camp, it will be open until eleven. Once I make sure things are going good I'll be back to sit and relax at the fire pit beside my camper. If you'd like to join me there, we can talk about this interesting development between us. Or talk about your upcoming camping trip needs."

She grinned. "I think I'll go back to my camper and get a wind jacket. It could get a little chillier the darker it gets. When I see your campfire near your trailer light up, I'll head over to join you and we'll talk."

He looked very pleased by her words. "That sounds great to me. I'll hurry."

CHAPTER NINE

Zane Tyson came out of the kitchen's walk-in freezer, carrying the platter of steaks he needed to prepare for the couple out on the porch. He caught Lisa finishing the salmon dishes she had been preparing. She placed them on their plates next to the sides and passed them to her waiting assistant to deliver.

"It's all yours." She relaxed against the counter.

He set his platter beside her. "Now that you finished those dishes, do you want to do these steaks? I'll step aside if you do. This is your kitchen, after all, but I'm hoping you'll relax for a few minutes." She had worked breakfast, then skipped lunch and returned for the dinner crowd. He had worked since lunch and was hanging out until the end of the night, as long as she needed him. He did not mind being here. He liked his boss. She wasn't only an excellent cook, but she was fun, with the way she talked to her people and the humor she brought to the room.

When she had first interviewed him, she'd been far more serious. The same after he'd taken the job. It was only lately that she'd lightened up, so he'd thought it might have just been her getting used to him. But then he'd overheard a conversation between her and Alice in Lisa's office one day. They were talking about her ex-husband, his new wife, and baby. From what he understood, the dude had started a secret affair with the woman, and they had a baby before Lisa had even known he was running around on her. It was disgusting and Zane felt sorry for her. She'd divorced her dumb ex and moved on.

Something had obviously happened recently, because she seemed happier and more outgoing with her kitchen people. Even him.

"Please, you do it, if you don't mind. I'm going to

check the crowd out there. Besides, I trust you completely."

"Thank you. That makes me happy. Now go have a little fun."

She didn't move, but smiled as he took his steaks out of their specialized sauce in which they'd been soaking. "You are doing an amazing job for me. I'm very grateful I have you."

His entire body swirled inside at her compliment. He hadn't been that gratified by praise in a long time. "I'm glad to be here, and I'm glad you're pleased. I'm happier about being here than I've been in a very long time. I think we make an excellent team."

She smiled widely. "I do too."

He watched her turn and walk out the door. He loved watching her walk so he just stood there watching her hips sway and her hair keep pace with them. Finally, he turned back to his steaks—his work. The thing she'd hired him to do. But as every day passed, he knew he was interested in her personally. However, she had hired him as her relief chef, and they worked opposite hours—never off at the same time until after they closed late and cleaned up the kitchen.

Becoming attracted to her was not a smart idea. And not why she'd hired him, so he kept his mouth shut. She had hired him for relief and good cooking. So that was what he would do.

He liked all the people who worked in the kitchen, and he liked the inn. And he loved the town and was thankful every day that he had seen that ad. He had become so bored with his life at the restaurant in Corpus. Though he loved the town, it was his life at the restaurant that had become lackluster. He had been so ready for something new. The restaurant owners wouldn't let him add anything new to the menu and had him train his assistants; they'd hired enough of them so they could always fill in for him. He'd been the advertised chef, however he no longer felt needed or interested. Not a good combination.

Here, it was different. He felt needed, and he was very interested. Now, he wasn't the number-one chef, but it didn't matter because he felt alive. Part of it was this beautiful, small town of Star Gazer Island, the beach that he lived on, and this inn and restaurant and this cooking crew. And his beautiful leader.

He flipped the steaks and smiled, happy about having moved here a short few months ago. And no matter how much he hadn't planned to crush on his new boss…he had.

* * *

Lisa walked out of the kitchen and ignored the thrill of talking with Zane. She tried not to call his name in her brain because she needed to stop feeling so alive when she was near him. He worked for her.

But the problem was, he sometimes made her feel special inside. These days, she did not want to feel special—not like that. Special as far as being a talented chef? Sure. That was what she worked so hard for. Why she was walking around out here in the dining room to visit with her customers and see whether anyone had any complaints about their food.

She wanted the restaurant's reputation to be great, so she would always work to fix problems. So far, she just hadn't had any. She walked around and spoke to customers who looked interested in speaking with her. To her pleasure, everyone complimented the food.

She moved out onto the deck, where she loved to eat; she gazed across the diners and spotted a man eating alone. He was watching her as she moved closer to him. She paused. He looked very familiar—oh goodness, she had dated him before she had met her awful ex-husband.

"Lisa," he said.

Walking forward, she smiled. "Stan. It's been awhile."

He smiled. "Yes, it has. How are you doing? Are you the chef here?"

"I'm doing good and yes, I'm the head chef. There's another chef who works here, too."

"This shrimp and pasta dish was wonderful. I could eat it every day I'm here."

She chuckled. "Well, you could if that's what you wanted to do, but there's a lot of wonderful food here. I tested it for weeks, worked hard on it before we ever opened the doors. Thank you for helping me know all the work was worth it."

"I had no idea when I booked this room that you were the chef. This is a great place to stay and to eat. I'd heard about it, so when I was passing through, I thought I would take a couple of nights off and relax, enjoy this beautiful shore. I'm glad I did."

"I'm glad you like it. It's nice seeing you." He had been a great guy.

"I heard you and your ex-husband have been divorced for a little while. I'm sorry about that and hope it didn't hurt you too horribly. But I never thought he was a good match for you."

She crossed her arms and gave a small shrug. "To be honest, I was so in love with him and now I don't even understand why. After what he did to me—I mean, going off and having a long affair and then a baby and still being married to me when I found out— I'm thankful I discovered it and took him to court. He got married right after we divorced. It killed any understanding of love fairly quickly for me. Now I just try not to think about it. And honestly, I love my life now. I love this restaurant, the beautiful view from here to the ocean, and the people who run this place and all of you customers who come in here to enjoy themselves."

His eyes seemed to light with interest.

The thought twisted her insides. Even so, he was a customer, and she came out to check on customers. "Where do you live?"

"I actually still live in San Antonio, where I moved not long after we stopped dating. I took a promotion with my sales company. But I'm traveling to Houston for a sales conference now and came down here for the weekend before I head up there tomorrow evening. I remember how nice it used to be. I had no idea I'd meet you here, but I'm glad."

"It's good to see you too."

"Do you have time to sit down for a few minutes?"

She didn't, although for a minute there she did kind of want to. "I'm sorry. I just came out for a minute to check on everybody and make sure that y'all are happy with everything. I've got to get back in there and help Zane cook. But it was nice to run into you again."

"I'll be here tomorrow, if you have any time off?"

She hesitated. "Um, I'll be working breakfast to about three o'clock."

"I can understand you might want to tell me no, but I would love it if you would have dinner with me. I'd enjoy a picnic on the beach and enjoy the view."

She hadn't done any of that sort of thing in so many years, but was she interested? She told herself he was a nice man, and it wasn't as if it were an actual date. They were just going to visit after all these years. "That sounds fun. I'll need to go home, take a shower, and get the food smell off me. So would five o'clock be okay?"

"Sounds perfect. I'll probably see you at breakfast in the morning too."

"I'm glad you enjoyed your meal. And if I don't see you at breakfast, we'll catch up at our dinner." She turned and headed back to the kitchen. As she walked through the inside dining area, she glanced out the glass door into the lobby and saw Alice wave for her. She went through the door to see what she needed.

"I was out on the deck a moment ago and you

really were having a long conversation with our guest," Alice said. "It looked nice."

"He and I dated right before I started dating my creepy ex-husband, and we haven't seen each other in years. He asked me if I would go for dinner on the beach with him tomorrow evening."

"You're going on a date. Wonderful."

"No, it's not a date. We're just visiting. He's a really nice guy who I dated like two or three times, but I quit dating him so I could start dating my ex, Mason. I obviously was insane back then. But if I'd been attracted enough to Stan, I wouldn't have stopped dating him. He's a nice man, though, so I'm going to dinner with him because we used to be friends."

Alice reached over and rubbed her arm. "I think that's a great idea, no matter what you call it. I'd love to hear what happens."

Lisa laughed. "I'll call you when I get home. Did you and Seth set a wedding date yet?"

"No. I can't believe it, but I am really thinking about it."

Lisa shook her head. "You were going to marry

him, whether or not you knew it, from day one. I'm just curious when that may be. I think everyone else is too, even your sons. But no rush, only whatever makes you and Seth happy." She winked, then turned and headed back to the kitchen.

She loved Alice. Alice had been so good to her by hiring her and letting her put her vision in this restaurant, so Lisa wanted the best for her. Finding Seth after she had been widowed was a good thing. And now maybe sweet happiness was going to come out on the other side.

CHAPTER TEN

Riley walked around the camp as fast as he could in order to get back to his fire pit and Sophie. What a surprise it had been to see her pull into the camp without any warning. If she'd wanted to surprise him, she'd done a great job.

Being his first weekend at the campground, her showing up made it even more special. Now he wanted to help her have a good evening and he wanted to get to know her better. He turned the corner of the office and saw her sitting in the chair on the other side of the fire pit. She smiled from beneath her black-and-white dotted blanket that she had wrapped around her.

"Hey," he said, as he walked up. "I have to say, I

like seeing you sitting there. And look at this, you got the fire going before I got back. Cool."

She chuckled, adding to her appeal. "I decided to come on over and get it ready for you. I camp enough that I know how to get campfires going."

"I can tell. Do you want something to drink? I have water and tea inside my camper. Or I can make some coffee really quick."

"Maybe a little glass of water just in case we talk so much I get dry in my mouth." She chuckled.

"Coming right up. I'd love to talk but don't want to give you a dry mouth."

He went inside to grab two glasses of ice water and then walked back outside and pushed the door closed with his foot. He handed her a glass and then sat down in the chair beside her. Leaning forward, he put his elbows on his knees as he looked at the fire, then her. "So here we are. You enjoy camping, obviously, since you've been doing it with all these nice ladies the last several years."

She looked up at the vast sky. "I do love it. It's just beautiful on a good day or a bad day, and especially with such a great group. A good day, a beautiful moon like tonight's, and tasty food make it perfect. Even if it is raining, we'll have a main meeting tent or better yet, use that metal roofed spot you've created, so we'll have a great time. I just know it."

He felt the same way. "I knew I would need it, so we started with a slab and roof. We'll add walls next if we decide it would be better."

"It sounds wonderful."

"Have you heard from the ladies who are coming?"

"Yes, and they are excited. The ones not getting to come are disappointed, so I think at the moment you are a success. I think it will be the same at the end of our third day when they get ready to leave. My feeling is they're going to love it because you're working so hard to make sure it's what they want. I appreciate that about you."

Her words curled through him in a really nice, warm way. "I'm trying to make sure I get that reaction."

"You're doing a superb job. Before you saw me at

that gas station, you never considered this?"

"Never crossed my mind. I was working at the ranch with all my brothers and carrying on my dad's legacy. But I had been getting restless before he died, but afterward my mind was on helping keep the ranch going like he would have wanted. Last year, I was getting restless again. My two older brothers were running everything with all the hired cowboys. My dad had always said if you want to work at the ranch you can, but if you find something else out there you want to do, then do it. And, as terrible as it is for me to say, my inheritance and part ownership gave me freedom to do what I wanted. And my brothers are all rooting me on."

"That's great. They all seemed happy for you."

"Yes, so hopefully I'll make a success of my obsession. And it's all been much more interesting to me since you showed up. This weekend and next weekend are giving families and couples time to enjoy together. But we're closed for the third weekend, with no campers. I will use that time to be ready for your ladies the next Friday, working on all those special things."

She smiled, and he loved it.

"Before you got everything figured out, was it hard for you, trying to decide?"

He shook his head. "No. Not at all. After listening to you at the gas station—that really made it clear what I wanted to try. It was easy to see that the manicures and massages were special to you and all the women you camped with so I was drawn to it. Yes, I'm a man, so it might be weird, but I kept thinking of my mom, and how she had lost my dad and was alone. She's not now, but I thought she might have enjoyed going camping with a bunch of women friends and having special treatments like massages while hanging out. You seemed to enjoy it so much from the short time we talked at the gas pump." He smiled at her, really glad she was sitting here at the campfire. "She really liked the idea, and as you know, she has her inn now and a special man who I think she's going to marry soon. But she says she's going to come out one weekend and camp. Who knows—it might be the weekend you and your friends come out here."

"I think that would be wonderful. And I think that,

as a man, you thinking about that is cool. I like that you didn't do it just to meet women."

"Okay, I'm not going to lie, I also hoped that I would meet you again. But that wasn't the only reason I wanted to open the camp. Women need a place to enjoy themselves. And then, lo and behold, before I even got it open you showed up and made my day. Heck, it's made my month...maybe my year." He laughed when she started to laugh. "Maybe I'm admitting too much."

"I think it's cool. Honestly, Riley, after not being attracted to anybody for a very long time, this is very interesting. I know it might not work out, but I'm having a splendid night. And it seems like you are too."

"I certainly am having a grand night. Had a great day. We're going to have a great day tomorrow, too." He would not rush this and run her off. He wanted to go over there and kiss her right now, but he wasn't going to—would not take the chance of moving too fast.

* * *

Sophie woke up the next morning in her cozy camper with Riley filling her thoughts. His smiling face had been in her mind all night. She got up, showered , then got ready and headed outside.

The morning was beautiful, with a soft sun rising that promised to be a pretty day. People were eating at the bar, but she had filled her little water bottle up before leaving the trailer and now headed out toward the beach. She loved jogging down the sand early in the morning with the beautiful ocean beside her. A man jogged toward her from the opposite end of the beach, and she smiled. He was smiling, too, as he drew up beside her. Her pulse had raced the moment she'd realized the man was Riley.

"Good morning, Sophie. I don't know why I didn't ask you last night if you jogged in the mornings. But I had already kept you up late enough, without trying to drag you out of bed too early."

She laughed and leaned her head to the side. "I do like to jog and got up a bit late this morning since last night someone kept me up talking about all kinds of things."

"Sorry about that. To make up for keeping you up so late, do you want to jog back and get some breakfast?"

She was so very tempted. "I think I'll finish jogging and let you do what you need to do this morning. I'm going to relax and see if I get any ideas to add to our camp. But any time you're free, just come grab me. I don't want to interrupt you when you need to do your boss man stuff, keeping everybody happy."

He grinned. "All right. Be safe and have fun. It's a nice jog."

"See you in a little bit." She watched him as he jogged off in his thigh-length shorts and no shirt. The man looked amazing. She turned away and continued jogging.

When she got back to the camp, she stopped by the breakfast area and bought a cup of coffee and a sausage wrap, then sat down at a table and enjoyed herself. Several people sitting around her were all talking, asking where everyone was from. She loved the way the four tables of people were chatting. They were all from nearby and had jumped on the beautiful new place near them to come. She wasn't sure how fast word would get out that Riley had started a glamping camp, but she was very sure the family camping would get out quickly. Everyone got up soon and headed off to the beach, and she ordered another cup of coffee.

"I'll take one too," Riley told the waitress as he walked up and sank into the chair across from her. "You look like you were really thinking."

"Actually, I was. I was thinking about you and your camp. I've been talking to a lot of the people sitting around. They are having a blast, and are all from around this area. So whether or not glamping works out for you, family camping is going to hit it off great. You can fill this place up with people."

"You don't think I'm going to make it with glamping?"

"No, that's not what I mean. I'm just looking at all categories, you know…what if something weird happens and you don't like glamping camp as much as you think you will? It won't be a big deal because you have all these families loving to come out. I'm just saying you have your choices."

"I agree, but with how much you and your group enjoy glamping, I believe I'm going to enjoy hosting a glamping weekend for you." He grinned and took a sip of coffee that had been delivered while they talked. "Did you enjoy your run?"

"Yes, it was lovely. And then I came here and ate a fantastic sausage and egg wrap and talked with your campers, and that's been wonderful."

"Great. I have to run into town and pick up a few things. Would you maybe want to go?"

"I'd enjoy that."

"You don't have to go—you may want to hang out and go to the beach or something. Your weekend is not geared around me."

He was a perfect host. "I realize that, but if I say no and watch you drive off, I'd be wishing I had gone with you." It was true.

He laughed and stood, then held his hand out to her.

She looked up at him, then slipped her hand into his. Instantly, a wonderful feeling raced up her arm.

Oh yes, she hadn't ever reacted to a man like she was to Riley.

CHAPTER ELEVEN

Lisa had gotten home, and showered and changed quickly into tennis shoes, jogging pants, and a teal-toned t-shirt. They were eating on the beach somewhere, so she hadn't dressed fancy. Which was good, because she didn't want him thinking this was a date.

Stan stopped by her house to pick her up, wearing knee-length black shorts and a tan shirt, looking as though he were ready to go golfing. Within minutes they were on the road, headed to the other end of the island's beach area. It was less congested and had trees and trails for walking.

"I actually haven't come down here since I started

working at the inn. But, years ago, I came out here a couple of times with friends. It's an interesting area."

"I was told about it and wanted to see it, so I drove out this morning and checked it out to make sure it was where I wanted to bring you. If you don't mind walking just a short distance before we open our basket for supper, I found a pretty spot."

"That will be great."

They walked through the trees. He carried the basket that held the blanket and whatever he had gotten them for dinner, and she walked beside him over some small trails. They came out to an area that was a little above the beach.

He smiled at her. "I walked down here and thought this was a nice place. And, no one else is sitting here, so it's ours."

"It's beautiful."

Stan set the basket down, then pulled the quilt out and spread it out on the grassy area. He set the basket in the middle and held out his hand. "Let me help you take a seat, madam."

Lisa took his hand and sank down on to the

blanket. He sat near her so they both faced the ocean view, but their nearness on the quilt made her uncomfortable. She hoped he didn't think she was interested in him again just because she agreed to come to dinner with him. "So you leave in the morning and go to Houston?"

He leaned forward and opened the lid of the picnic basket. "I do. I have to be there by two in the afternoon, so I'll be heading out early. I'm glad to have a bit of rest here because when I get to the conference, I'll be busy. It's been a major pleasure to run into you while I was taking a break." He'd pulled several white food containers from the basket while he talked, then handed her an iced-down drink in a metal container. "Having dinner with you has made this a great trip. I hope this is all good for you. Tea is unsweet like you like, and there is an iced-down bottle of wine in there if you wanted some."

Lisa's nerves were rattled a bit. "Thank you for bringing it, but I really don't want any. The tea is perfect." She needed her brain in perfect working order. She drank wine every once in a while, and enjoyed it, but right now she didn't want to take any chance of altering her mind's thinking process.

"Whatever you want." Stan opened the two containers of food from a restaurant in town that had great lasagna, which was what he'd brought. "I hope you like this. I tried to remember what you'd eaten when we went out, and this was what came to mind."

"You remembered right. This restaurant has fantastic Italian food. I've only eaten there a couple of times, but their lasagna is wonderful."

"Perfect."

The smell was great, and his memory was startling. Lisa actually didn't remember a lot about their few dates, and if he hadn't mentioned lasagna, she wouldn't have remembered they'd eaten it. She thought about it for a minute and remembered he'd taken her to a movie and dinner, then home. Stan started to kiss her on their first date at her front door, but she'd turned her face, so he kissed her on the cheek. She'd hurried inside, feeling bad that she hadn't kissed him after he'd tried so hard to give her a good night. When he'd called for another date, she'd said okay, wanting to give him another chance because he was a nice guy.

However, the night before their second date, she met her now ex-husband Mason. And as crazy as it sounded now, she had been instantly drawn to him. Sadly, she knew on the second date with Stan that there was no future between them. She thanked him when he brought her home, then told him she'd been invited out by someone else and had accepted. She apologized but just didn't feel drawn to him. He'd looked hurt but wished her the best.

Now here they were, eating in a picturesque spot. She again hoped he wasn't thinking this was a date, a new beginning. If he was, she would let him know immediately that she was honored, but that she wasn't dating anyone now—maybe ever.

Not after what she had been through.

As they ate, he asked her about running the restaurant and whether she'd stay here in this town or open a new one somewhere else.

"I'm not opening one anywhere else. I'm going to stay here in this town and work with my good friend

Alice, building this inn up. I'm very happy."

"I see. If I wanted to date you again, I guess I could just drive down from San Antonio and spend the night at the inn and take you out."

Her stomach rolled. Thankfully, this part of the conversation had come at the end of the meal. "I should have told you yesterday that I was just coming on the picnic to visit with you since we go way back. But I'm not here to date anyone. I'm past dating, after my awful divorce. I ran off to Europe for a few months after it was over, then I came back, determined not to run away anymore. Alice was a long time friend looking for a chef for her new restaurant she was opening. I went to see her and felt automatically drawn to the inn and restaurant. She hired me on the spot when I asked about it. I hadn't been that happy in a very long time. So here I am now, thoroughly enjoying myself, and I'm not doing anything that could mess that up. I came out to dinner with you as an old friend. Now I see I should have clarified that to you in the beginning. I'm sorry."

Stan had looked out at the water halfway through

her words. Now he looked back at her. "I understand. I guess I was just thinking maybe this could be our time since last time got interrupted by him."

She could tell him that her ex had nothing to do with her stopping their dating. He was still a nice man and they could be friends. But she had to be honest. "No. I'm sorry. I liked you back then as a friend, but wasn't going out with you again whether or not I went out with anyone else. So, like I said, I came to lunch with you as an old friend. Not as a date. Just two old friends getting together. And I wish you all the luck in the world tomorrow at your conference."

He sighed. "Thank you. I hope your future is just exactly how you want it to be."

"I wish the same thing for you."

After Stan dropped her off at her house, they parted with a gentle hug. Lisa closed the door, ending their evening. She went out onto the back porch, satisfied that she'd made the right choice.

Her thoughts went to Zane. She glanced over toward her restaurant, which was now closed for the night. She was quite certain he had done an excellent job. That was just the man he was—a skilled cook and a…very handsome, thoughtful, and nice man.

And she did not need to think about Zane like this. She was not interested in men.

And yet he seemed different. Going out tonight with Stan seemed to make Zane's differences jump out at her.

CHAPTER TWELVE

When Sophie and Riley reached Star Gazer Island, he drove to the grocery store to get a few things the cooks had requested. "Do you want to come in, or are you going to wait in the truck? I'll just need a few spices and products the kitchen team has run out of. I'll order more next time."

"I'm going inside with you. Who knows, I may want some ice cream or something."

He laughed. "That will be fine. I'll share it with you, if you're serious."

"Perfect. I love this area and I really like it down here."

"I have to say, I wish that feeling had something

to do with me."

She grinned at him, then got out of the truck.

He strode quickly around the front of the truck and smiled at her. "I'm serious, but I understand I'll have to aim for next time." He winked at her as they walked beside each other through the wide doorway.

"You're doing a good job," she said, in a way that had his excitement flying.

He grabbed a basket. The small items—butter, spices, and some other items that the cook had written on a piece of paper for him—would be hard to handle in his hands. They walked up and down several aisles and were at the refrigerated area to grab the butter when he saw his mother.

"Mom, what a surprise. How are you doing this morning?"

Alice looked up from what she was studying on the back of a package of butter. "Riley, it's so great to see you." She threw her arms around him and they hugged each other. Her gaze locked with Sophie's and she let go Riley. "Sophie, oh my goodness, it is so good to see you again."

Sophie threw her arms around Alice. They hugged tightly and then stepped back, smiling. "It's nice to see you again too. I came down to the camp this weekend. You know, testing it out for my group that's coming at the end of the month."

His mom's smile was enormous. "Wonderful. And you're hanging out with my son. I think that's fabulous. You know, the guy doesn't date much lately, so seeing him hanging out with a woman is really nice. Sorry—don't mean to embarrass you or anything. I don't even know if there's anything between the two of you. But seeing you this morning was unexpected and…I'm rattling on when I should hush and not say things I shouldn't. I'm excited you're back, checking out everything. I'm thinking Riley is too."

Riley almost laughed at her obvious excitement at seeing them together. His gaze flew to Sophie's and saw she was fighting off laughter too. "Mom, please, we have this handled."

Sophie placed a hand on his arm. "Your son is a great guy, and I thank you for sounding like you would approve if he was dating me."

"I certainly would. He is a very wonderful fella and anyone who wanted to date him would be a smart woman. But it's none of my business. Okay, I have buy Lisa her butter—she's run out of it in the restaurant and I need to get it to her. Then I'm picking up Lorna and the baby and we're heading out to the ranch to have lunch with Nina so I'll head out now."

"You have a good day planned. Have fun."

"I will. You two have fun too." She grinned and then headed out.

"She's thrilled that you might be dating somebody."

"Yes." It felt really odd standing in the grocery store discussing this. "She normally doesn't say much. But I think she noticed something different when I had dinner with you last weekend, and she likes you."

"It's fine with me, although you and I are both going at this cautiously."

He took a step closer to her. Anybody passing by could see them standing next to the butter. And he figured he looked as if he wanted to kiss her, and he did. "I'm being very cautious, if you've noticed how hard it is for me not to have kissed you yet."

"I've noticed. And I think that when the time is right, it will happen."

He sighed. "Just to let you know, my brain keeps urging me that it's time, but I'm not kissing you in the middle of the grocery store. So, I guess we better head back to camp."

"You're a very smart man. A grocery store is not the ideal place to have a first kiss."

He looked over his shoulder at her. "You don't think this is the most romantic place in the world?"

"Not exactly." She chuckled.

The sound raced through him like the tingle of excitement at the thought that pretty soon it would happen, and no matter where they were, the kiss would make it a very romantic place.

Alice had been shocked and happy to run into Riley and Sophie at the store. Maybe something good was happening there. She thought about it as she drove out to pick up Lorna and the baby at their ranch and the baby quickly took her thoughts to spending the afternoon with him and her daughter-in-laws.

Now they were walking through the side door of what used to be her and William's ranch home. Now it was Jackson and Nina's home. Alice had loved her life here with her husband and sons. But now God had given her a new life, owning her Star Gazer Inn, where she'd met William for the first time and now where she'd met Seth. She'd had to accept life—the way it brought happiness, took it away, and then gave it again. That didn't always mean with love again, but just a new way of life to help a person smile. She'd been unexpectedly blessed with that—and also with love from Seth.

And her sons were being blessed with love and that, too, blessed her. When Nina had called and invited her and Dallas's wife and baby to come out for an afternoon visit, Alice accepted instantly. Nina wanted them to give their opinion on her new art and on the puppies they had rescued on the side of the road.

Alice was carrying Landon as they walked inside.

She loved the little fella and hoped that Nina would call her soon with the news that she and Jackson were expecting a baby. Instead, her call had been about puppies. But puppies were lovely too. As they walked inside, Nina's adorable Goldendoodle, Buttercup, came around the corner. Two small, probably less than three months old, puppies followed the fluffy, happy leader. Behind all of them was a smiling Nina.

"Oh my goodness, they are so precious." Lorna bent down to pet the beautiful older puppy, and the new very young ones dove at her. She laughed and took one in each arm. Buttercup sat and looked from one to the other too, as if she were insulted by them taking the woman's attention from her.

Alice watched the show and thought it was cute.

"They are adorable." Lorna looked at the puppies.

Alice knelt also, letting Landon lean forward in her arms, trying to reach the pups in his mom's arms. His legs wiggled to get down; he had reached the age where he was almost ready to walk. She held onto him though, not sure about the pups yet.

Nina chuckled. "I think so too. And it looks like

Landon does as well. We rescued them on the way home from the airport. They were just outside the entrance to the ranch."

"It's been about two weeks, right?" Alice asked.

"Yes, and despite all the notices we've put out, nobody has made one claim for them. Which leads me to wondering if we are going to keep them or if someone we know might take a liking to one of them—or both of them. We had thought that they could become cow dogs like Shep and Socks, our two outside dogs that love playing with them. But we've both been looking at them, and though we don't know what breed they are, we don't think they're going to be very big, or good cattle dogs. I mean, we've had them for two weeks and they haven't grown hardly at all." She looked at Lorna and her lips curved.

Lorna smiled, understanding Nina's intentions, and she looked back at her son. He kept pulling his hand back from touching the pups and then would try again.

Alice could tell he wanted to touch them so badly and continued to let him reach out.

Lorna shifted the puppies so they could lick his hands and he giggled.

Alice did too, loving the joy in his giggle. "He looks like he'd love one."

Lorna looked at her and nodded. "With the way he's reacting, it might be nice to have a small, friendly puppy for him to play with. Most of the time, he just has himself, me, and Dallas. But he sees mostly me during the days. I'll take a couple of days to think about it and ask Dallas. I wouldn't want to make a wrong decision, but I think this little gold one is going to be the smallest one. And he's very sweet."

Alice agreed, but let the conversation be between her daughters-in-law.

"I totally agree on your choice." Nina smiled at her. "We're going to have them out here for forever probably, unless someone feels the draw to claim them. And I thought about Landon instantly. If y'all decide you want him, just let me know. And I haven't named them yet, in case you might want to name the pup. I think either puppy would work well for Landon, but my first thought went to the littlest one."

Landon laughed as he tried to reach the pups again since Alice had pulled him back a bit.

Lorna chuckled, watching him. "Thank you for thinking of us, Nina. Don't you think it's a good idea, Alice?"

"Very much so," Alice agreed happily.

Nina grinned. "Great. So now that we have a puppy plan, would y'all please come into my office and give me your opinions about the art that's going in the next exhibit?"

Alice couldn't wait to see Nina's new paintings. They followed her down the hall to the six walls of glass. Alice had loved to raise flowers in this room and to play with her sons in here. Nina had made it her art studio, and it was perfect. When they walked into the large room, she stopped instantly. There were three heart-stopping paintings finished and facing them.

The first painting was one of Nina's normal ocean-type views—always stunning, but this one had beautiful bright waves and a pretty rock protruding from the water down the coast. A two-story home sat along the way, with a rising sun behind it highlighting the water, the rock, and the house.

The second portrait was of a pasture from this ranch. It had horses grazing and a little boy chasing after a colt and two puppies chasing after him. He was very young, a little older than Landon, wearing jeans and a red shirt, with his arms up in the air and a big smile on his face. It was a heart-grabbing painting that drew Alice strongly.

Then the third picture was one of the things Nina was known for—a beautiful ocean scene with a gorgeous sun beaming as it began setting. It was breathtaking, with its multiple tones of pink, blue, and golds sparkling and reflecting on the water.

Amazing. Gorgeous. Touching.

She and Lorna both were silent as they studied the pictures. Now, she looked at Lorna, and Lorna looked at her; they both smiled and then turned to look at Nina.

"Outstandingly wonderful," Alice managed breathlessly.

Lorna put her hand out and touched Nina's arm. "I have no words other than they are so touching. It's as if you completely captured all of this."

"Obviously your show is going to be a combination of your Western paintings and your ocean because you are so talented at both," Alice said. It wasn't a question because it was true.

Nina's expression relaxed with apparent relief. "Yes. My manager is thrilled because he wanted me to blend the two different types of special art focus and so I am."

"That's wonderful," Alice said. "And are you having more than just the three, or is it in with some other artist?"

"Those five there on the wall go too, but you've seen them since I was working on them last time you were over. It's kind of mind-blowing to me, realizing that so many people have missed my paintings while I was out. My manager has upped my prices even higher, and it's a bit startling."

"It is very well deserved. You've been working on these for several months. And you actually shocked me with how quickly you can produce an astounding piece of artwork." Lorna smiled at Nina.

Alice knew she meant every word. "I'm in total agreement. You are so amazing, and I love that this room I always enjoyed so much has a new, wonderful life now."

"Thank you both." Nina looked even more relieved. "I trust you two and knew you would be very honest. It shows on your faces. I can now call my agent to come out and take a look, or I can send her a picture from my phone if she wants a quicker look. She'll be thrilled. And I'm relieved, and Jackson will be too, since he knew I value his opinion and both of yours."

They all hugged and Alice was thrilled with the connection she had with her two sons' wives.

Nina smiled. "Let's head out to the patio so the pups can run free and we can enjoy a beautiful lunch. I can celebrate with you two."

Happily, they headed out. Alice and the baby followed behind her daughters-in-law. Her thoughts went to Riley and the beautiful Sophie, who she thought was a splendid match for him. She wondered what was happening with them right now on the beach.

Alice couldn't help but feel blessed with

everything going on around her.

* * *

After getting back to the camp, Sophie and Riley had a meal at the beach restaurant. She still didn't know what to call it—a bar, restaurant, or diner…or something else. It was a delightful place, and bar just didn't seem right. They ordered steak baskets that were great. As was her handsome company.

She wasn't surprised to see that many of the people had dinner at their little campfires beside their campers and tents. Because of that, the camp's small restaurant wasn't horribly crowded.

"I see you looking around. Are you thinking about how many of them are eating at their campers and tents? I wasn't expecting as many people to enjoy cooking at their campfire. Especially once you taste the food served at this nice outdoor seating café slash snack bar. The food is great. I can't imagine wanting to cook hot dogs or hamburgers when you can have all these choices."

"It's their love of cooking in the outdoors. At our

camp, we provide them two fun evening meals with their payment, and we spend the time visiting, listening to music and having a great time. But this is really cool, look at how much fun they all seem to be having—it's a great family event."

"I think so, too. I keep looking around at all these kids and the joy on their faces and how much fun they're having."

His voice had trailed off, and she sensed he was thinking about the families. "Are you going to have a family one day?" she asked, suddenly needing...wanting to know.

He grinned at her. "I want to have kids very much one day. Obviously, the time hasn't come so far. Since you haven't dated in a very long time, do you think about having kids?"

Her nerves shook. "I used to when I first started dating. But after dating for so long and no man tempting me to marry, much less have babies, I pushed the want out of my thoughts when I started camping instead of dating. But for many years I totally thought I'd have at least two children. I haven't kissed a man

138

or thought of marrying a man in over five years. I figure if God wants me to marry, He'll send the man, and if He wants me to have kids, He would make it happen. In the meantime, I've busied myself with other things like camping, helping women in similar situations like mine have fun."

"Do you feel any kind of positive thoughts about us?"

Her heart slammed against her ribs. This wonderful man was kind, enthusiastic, and caring, and she was drawn to everything about him. He was also sexy, tempting, and drew every ounce of her heart's desire. "I think with how I'm drawn to you…that we could truly have a future. I wouldn't have agreed to date you if I hadn't seen some kind of potential."

"I like the sound of that, because I feel the same way. I don't see how I could have such powerful feelings toward you so quickly, but my brothers fell for their wives quickly too. But anyway, I didn't want you to think that I was just messing around with you. I haven't even kissed you and in all honesty, I'm about to go crazy because I want to so bad."

Her body trembled at his words. "What should we do—go to the campfire with everybody and listen to the music, or go for a moonlight walk?"

"My vote is a moonlight walk, and I'm going to kiss you." His eyes were warm and inviting.

Fifteen minutes later, he was holding Sophie's hand as they walked down the ocean beach. When they had gotten far enough away from the sound of everyone laughing, clapping, and having a good time, he stopped walking, slipped his arms around her, and pulled her close.

Sophie's insides shivered with excitement, want, and delight as he lowered his lips to hers…and totally set her world on fire.

* * *

Riley had never felt so alive as he did kissing Sophie. The kiss was long and deep, soft and tender. It took everything in him to tug his lips from hers, realizing she was having just as much trouble as he was. He leaned his forehead to hers and breathed in a deep breath of air as she did the same.

"I've never experienced anything like your kiss," he said at last. It was so true. "I think we better head back while we can still walk."

She chuckled and nodded. "I agree. Though that's not exactly what I want."

"We agree on everything." He pulled his head back and stared at her. "You've made this first camp a great beginning." He knew he wanted to keep her forever, but he dared not say that yet. They needed more time. And why not? Every moment they spent together was wonderful. There was no rush. He wasn't taking any chance of running her off because he felt so tempted to fall on his knee and propose to her here and now.

By the end of the next day, when he hugged her and told her good-bye, he had a really hard time ending the kiss and then watching her smile and wave as she drove away.

All he wanted to do was race after her.

CHAPTER THIRTEEN

On Sunday evening, Zane walked out of the freezer, having put the last supplies inside. It was only nine o'clock but on Sunday nights they closed early, at eight, and he liked having a night he got off early. Tonight, he and Lisa had both worked, and he had enjoyed it. But he was still curious about the man she had gone to dinner with yesterday afternoon. When he had gotten off last night, it had looked like she was home because the lights were all on at her place, but he wasn't positive, and it was ten-thirty when he locked the doors and headed to his truck. He was tempted to check on her, but he wouldn't let himself. He would admit it was getting harder and harder to resist checking on her.

It was something he felt she wouldn't welcome. Although sometimes he got the impression that she might be interested in him. However, if that were the case, she fought it off very well.

When he walked back into the kitchen area, everybody had already left, and she wasn't in the kitchen. He walked over to her open office door and found her sitting behind her desk. He leaned his shoulder against the door and crossed his arms as she looked up from the computer. She was beautiful.

"They're all gone. How are you doing this evening?" He'd asked her the same question this morning when she got to work, but she had said she was fine. She had been quieter than usual all day, and it made him wonder.

She leaned back, took a deep breath, and then let it out slowly as she held his gaze. "I'm fine."

"You sure are quiet."

"Maybe. I think I'm going to go for a walk on the beach."

"It's dark out there."

"I do that sometimes. Alice goes with me some, but not tonight. I think she went over to Seth's house for a little while."

"Would you mind if I walked with you?"

She bit her lip, then stood. "Sure, if you want to. I have to stop by the house and put my tennis shoes on, though."

Excitement rolled through him. "I need to get mine out of my truck. I'd wear these chef shoes, but I don't care to wear them in the sand."

"Then I guess we'll head that way."

"I'll drive you to your house, if you want me to."

"Thanks, but by the time you walk out there all the way to your truck and then drive me to my house, I'd already be home and have changed. See you in a few minutes. Come through the back gate and I'll be on my back porch."

"Sounds good."

They locked the door, and he went one way and she went the other.

Moments later, he walked through the back fence and around the corner, and saw her sitting on the back porch. She had quickly changed into a pair of long shorts, a t-shirt, and a pair of tennis shoes. And she pulled her mid-length hair into a ponytail.

"Are you ready to walk? I know I am." He smiled.

She smiled as she stood. "More than ready. Let's hit it."

They walked out the back fence and across the sand to where the sand was harder and could handle jogging shoes—not the wet sand next to the water rolling in.

"It's pretty out here in the moonlight, isn't it?"

She looked at him and nodded as they walked. "I've been enjoying this since I moved here. It's wonderful to walk along the shore first thing in the morning and in the evening."

He had placed his hands in his pockets and slid her a sideways glance. "Do you run into a lot of people early? Or at this hour?"

"There's usually not many people. I know what you're probably thinking—that it is a bit dangerous early or late, but it's been fine. I haven't run into anybody who looks like they want to attack me.

There's a lot of houses up and down this area, and it feels safe to me."

He wasn't so sure about that, and would start worrying about her all the time. "Well, anytime you need somebody to walk with you, just ask." He was probably saying more than he needed to say, but he couldn't help it.

"Thank you, but I can take care of myself. So, the house that you rented—it's on the water, too, isn't it?" She had obviously redirected the discussion.

"Yes, on the opposite side of town. It's not that far a drive. I mean, it would be a little far of a walk to work, but I jog it for exercise. It's at the end of a side street, just right past the feed store on Main Street. I like it a lot and bought it, actually. I'm settling here." He smiled at her shocked expression. He'd decided almost instantly this was the right place for him.

"I'm stunned, but that's great. That lets me know you really do like your job."

"Yes, I do. And the people I work with and my boss. I'm fifty and ready to find a place where I want to settle down. I knew this was it the moment I arrived and interviewed with you. The town appealed to me—the restaurant and such a talented boss."

She stared at him, startled. "Well." She paused and cleared her throat. "I have to agree with you. This is where I'm going to settle down. I haven't bought a house yet, but I love the one I'm renting beside the inn. Alice is going to have to run me off if she wants to get rid of me because I'm not leaving on my own. I really enjoy it out here on the beach. I love my work. I work with a lot of really nice people, including you, and as far as I know, I'm here to stay."

He reached down and picked up a rock for something to do. He turned toward the ocean and threw the rock out to sea in the darkness. His mind was fighting over whether to ask what he wanted to ask her—about the man from yesterday—or to keep his mouth shut. He tried to talk himself out of asking her about the date—it didn't work.

He turned toward her in the moonlight. "How did your date go yesterday, if you don't mind me asking?"

She picked up a shell and held it for a minute. "I didn't look at it as a date, and I told him that." She

147

tossed the shell out into the ocean, then took a deep breath. "He was someone I dated a couple times, a long time ago. I had decided not to go out with him again and was going to tell him on our second date that we had already planned for that coming Friday. I met my ex the night before the date and accepted a date with him on Saturday night. I broke up with Stan the next night as planned, and then Mason and I went out the following night and married less than a year later. The marriage was so fast and our life was so busy, with his career taking off rapidly, that finding out about his cheating was a shock. I wanted a divorce and he wanted a divorce, so it was done in short order. The news got around fairly quickly that I divorced Mason.

"When Stan arrived here and saw me, not realizing I worked here, he evidently thought we could start over. I told him I wasn't leaving here, that I wasn't ever getting married, that I was fine the way I was, and he acted like he really didn't understand." She frowned and her eyes glinted in the moonlight. "And that bothers me when men don't understand. Anyway, he left and knows I'm not open to dating or moving."

Zane took in what she had said. What he had thought was true: she had no plans to remarry. Or date.

Really, if you would never marry, you weren't even going to take a chance on a romance starting, right? Besides, they worked opposite hours; they'd never have days off together. The only time they could ever be together would be before work or after. So why was he disappointed that she would never be available? But she was the only one who'd interested him in a really long time.

"Does that sound crazy on my part?" She stared at him.

He lifted his shoulder in a shrug. "Not really, after what you've been through. However, you could be closing off your future. I know people who were cheated on and divorced and later on, sometimes almost immediately, they met the love of their life. They continued on and have had a wonderful relationship, thankful for the mess their husband or wife put them through, enabling them to meet the actual person they were meant for." He hoped it could happen for her.

Looking shocked and confused, she started walking again, and he fell into step with her. She glanced at him. "I just don't think that will ever happen. Although sometimes I think about it."

Zane had the funniest feeling she was talking about him, because several times he'd caught her looking at him. He got that warm feeling and in that moment, his mood jumped with hope.

CHAPTER FOURTEEN

Jackson and Nina pulled up in front of Dallas and Lorna's house. He smiled over at Nina. "All right, are you ready to give the puppy away?"

"I am. I think that this sweet little ball of fur is going to be a great puppy to grow up with Landon. And Lorna actually sounded really excited about getting it when she called and said they did want it."

"Then let's do this."

They climbed out of the truck. She carried the soft golden puppy to the sidewalk and then put him down to run around in the grass for a moment just in case it needed to go to the restroom. It did and then raced to the kitchen door just as a smiling Lorna opened it.

"I've been waiting, and I'm so excited you're here," she said, as Nina picked up the puppy before it could run into the house.

"We're glad to be here," Nina said as Lorna happily rubbed the pup's head.

"Landon is sitting in his playpen. He's not quite up to walking yet, so I thought that would be a good place for him for this first meeting. He's sitting close to the outside edge, so he'll be able to see the puppy really well, or maybe even touch it through the netting with his fingertips. Or if you think it's better for me to hold him, I'll do that. Honestly, I'm a bit nervous about what to do."

He smiled at his sister-in-law. "Don't be nervous. We'll go with your plan of Landon being in the playpen, and if they seem to get along, which I believe they will, then take him out and put him on the floor with the puppy. I think they're going to be buddies. Have you come up with a name for him?"

"I haven't thought about it yet. But they are going to be buddies so Buddy sounds good. Look at the little fella—he's just grinning at me." She smiled at the pup.

"Hey, little Buddy, I think you're going to fit in really well. You look like you're going to be small, which will make you being tucked inside the house with us perfect. Now come meet your little play pal."

They walked into the house and she bent down to show the puppy to Landon, who immediately started waving his hands at the puppy. The door opened and Dallas walked in.

"Come on in," Jackson said, grinning. "Your baby is falling in love with the puppy."

"Great. Look at that grin. It's just like you hoped, Lorna." He watched Lorna hold the wiggling puppy as a happy Landon stuck his fingers through the netting to touch him.

"He loves the pup. I think we can take him out of the pen."

Nina looked at Lorna. "Can I hold Landon? I am so glad to see him, and I want a baby so bad."

Lorna nodded. "He would love for you to hold him, and I'll take care of this puppy dog as they get to know each other. You fellas can do whatever y'all want to do right now."

"Come on, we'll let them have the fun of playing with the puppy while I show you my colts." Dallas started toward the door.

"Sounds good. Y'all have fun." Jackson followed his brother. He'd been wanting to see the colts his brother was training and selling so well lately. Marrying Nina had been the best move Jackson had made, and his brother marrying Lorna had been his best move.

They walked into the morning sunshine, happy their wives were inside having fun. "We did good, marrying two women who like each other." He grinned at Dallas.

He grinned too. "Yes, we did."

* * *

After the husbands closed the door behind them, Nina reached down and picked up the adorable little boy, who immediately put his hand on her face. "Hello, sweetie pie. One day, you're going to be able to say Aunt Nina." She kissed his cheek; he grinned at her and patted her face again. She glanced at Lorna. "I think he likes people holding him."

Lorna looked up. "Yes, he does. I'm very grateful for him, so I tend to hold him more than I should. Anytime you want to take him to your house and play with him, I'll let you."

"That sounds like a good plan." Nina eased back down to sit on the floor with her adorable nephew. "I can be his aunt, and let you and Dallas go out to dinner. Let's do that this week."

Lorna chuckled. "That's a great idea. Thank you for suggesting we get Buddy. He fits in perfectly."

"Wonderful." Nina watched the tiny puppy and baby interact. "I love watching them."

"I do too. So, how's it going with you getting pregnant?"

She sighed. "So far, no luck. But I'm not giving up. Holding this sweet boy gives me determination not to lose hope."

Lorna touched her arm. "It will happen. I know it will."

"Me too." She prayed her feelings were right. It

was the only way she was going to let her thoughts go right now. She looked at Landon. He was such an adorable baby and made her want her own child even more. She would do whatever it took to have a baby—slow down her painting career if she needed to—just to hold her and Jackson's baby.

"You're so lucky to have this beautiful little baby. And I know Dallas is so happy that he met you and helped save Landon being born. I'm really jealous of you getting to hold him every day and imagining bringing him up. Me and Jackson want it so much. We've been trying since January. I haven't told Jackson, but I'm getting a little worried that maybe something's wrong with one of us."

"Don't get upset right now. Y'all just started trying, really. Sometimes it just takes a little while. Then sometimes, like me, I have been single all this time and I'm not one to sleep with a guy—I don't even know why I did with a guy like Lewis, who I barely knew. It was craziness on my part, and then I got pregnant immediately. And then he died, but I had this beautiful little baby, and Dallas rescued me and we fell in love. What I'm saying is sometimes you don't know what wonderful miracle God has planned. Maybe it will happen naturally, or maybe you'll need the help of some doctors. Or maybe you'll be able to adopt. God has a plan, and you two will find out what it is. But right now, you just started. I mean, y'all have only been married since December, so you haven't been trying for horribly long. So just relax and let the Lord take control. I've just learned that myself, and He sent me Dallas, the love of my life, to be my husband and Landon's father. It will happen. And if it doesn't, then y'all know you're supposed to try something new."

"Thanks for the encouragement. And thank you for having this adorable little boy." She stood and walked him around the room, bouncing him on her hip. "I don't doubt Jackson isn't out there talking to Dallas about it all too. He knows I'm kind of getting obsessed about getting pregnant and it probably worries him for me. He accepts that the baby will come when it's supposed to, and if it doesn't, then we'll do whatever it takes to have one or adopt one. But anyway, I guess I'm jumping the gun, like he tells me. So now, I'm just going to enjoy myself this morning."

"Great, relaxing will probably be good for you. This puppy is just so fun—he's going to be a great friend to Landon. So what are you going to do with the other little pup?" Lorna asked.

"We don't know yet. We haven't decided if we'll keep him or keep hunting for someone to love him."

"If I hear that somebody wants another puppy do you want me to tell them you have one?"

"Sure, you can tell them and then call me, and I'll tell you if I'm going to keep him."

"Sounds good. What do you think about our mother-in-law and her boyfriend? Do you think she's going to keep him?"

Nina smiled at Lorna's words. "Yes. I am happy for her and I am so ready for those two sweethearts to decide to get married. I think she might be considering it."

"That's exactly what I think. I talked to her briefly the other day about it and she told me they were thinking about speeding it up."

"That's almost exactly what she told me. I hope

our men are truly ready for their mom to remarry."

"I think they are. But if we decide they aren't, then we need to prepare them, because it's coming."

"I think it will be great. And that will give this little baby boy a grandma and a grandpa to love him. When Jackson and I finally have ours, it will be the same. To see two people like them, who have both been through the loss of their truly loved wife and husband, I think this is wonderful."

"I do too."

Nina smiled at her sister-in-law, her friend, and felt grateful to have her. "It will be fun helping Alice with her wedding."

"Yes, it will be. And I'm hoping that I'll be holding a baby shower for you soon."

"That would be a dream come true." Nina's heart went wild at the idea.

CHAPTER FIFTEEN

The day of the glamping camp, Sophie got there first thing in the morning, pulling her trailer. She was excited and so ready to see Riley again. They had talked on the phone several times, but he had been so busy getting the camp ready the last two weeks and she had been swamped with several appraisals in the opposite direction of Star Gazer Island that there had been no time to see each other.

That made today even more special. She was the first to arrive and halted her Jeep next to his office. She saw him across the way with a couple of cowboys in the area they had set up to hold the horses. They were temporary holdings and could be taken down after the weekend was over, since the regular campers wouldn't get this nice paid-for event.

She climbed out of the Jeep just as he spotted her. He smiled, said something to the guys, and then headed her way. Her heart raced as she watched him cross the way toward her. She had thought about him for the last two weeks. He didn't even halt as he strode to her, took her hand, and led her to the other side of his office, then engulfed her in his arms and kissed her.

She melted against him and kissed him back. Warmth and joy filled her, and she was completely overtaken with what she felt for him. It was something she had never felt in her life. Could it be love? That was what she'd suspected since she'd left two weeks ago.

If she was completely honest with herself, it was what she wanted. Her life since meeting him here at the camp at the beginning of the month had been different than it ever had been. And she now had three camp days with him again.

He pulled back and smiled at her; she smiled back at him. "Hello. I love being greeted by you."

He touched her face with his fingertips, still holding onto her with his other arm. "I can't help myself. I've had you on my mind since you left, and I could barely stand the time it took to see you again so I could kiss you again. I'm crazy about you."

She leaned her head against his shoulder. "And I'm crazy about you too." She angled back and studied him. "But I'm assuming that only in private moments can we show this much adoration for each other. The rest of the time, we're just friends. We don't want to give everyone the wrong idea."

"What is the wrong idea? Because I'm crazy about you, so if that's the idea they get, it's not wrong."

"No, that's not what I mean. I don't want them to think I picked this beautiful place because I'm crazy about you. I want them to get an opinion of this place on their own, and then later we can be open about what we feel for each other. Who knows? By that time, you may be ready to get rid of me."

He threw his head back and laughed, then gave her a point-blank look. "I doubt that will happen, so I'm giving you a warning."

Her stomach trembled. "To be honest with you, I like the sound of that."

They agreed, it seemed like, and only time would tell whether he was as thick in feelings for her as she was for him.

She stepped back from him and then waved toward her vehicle. "Okay, so where can I park?"

He pointed to the closest parking area to his trailer, about twenty feet away. He lifted an eyebrow in question.

She stared at the spot, wanting so badly to take it but thinking of maybe a reason she shouldn't have it. Then she realized she was in charge of the weekend, as he was, and them being near each other might be a good thing.

"I think that's a good thought since we'll both be looking over everybody. You won't have to come hunting me down most times when we're out and about."

"I totally agree."

She chuckled; it was easy to see the twinkle in his eyes. She headed toward her Jeep and within moments had parked her little camper in its spot. He unhooked it from her Jeep, and she pulled it around and parked next to the camper.

They walked around the camp, and she admired the layout. The area for the massage and manicurist was all organized, and it looked great.

By one o'clock, they had the registration table set up with the sign-in and trailer assignments. Everybody could get signed in, know where to park their camper, and park—or to have Riley park it for them. Sneaky Riley had left the spot he suggested to her vacant in case she would take it, so it didn't mess up the assignments.

As usual, soon after lunch, ladies began to arrive. Normal arrival was finished by around six o'clock. Dinner was at seven o'clock, so they all tried to arrive by then.

He had hired a country singer from the area to come in for the greeting party and sing and that, too, was included in their payment. Everything he had done was fairly reasonable, but the ladies were all accustomed to the cost and it was not much more than four nights at a nice hotel. And if they wanted the extra massages other than the one that was included in the cost, then they paid on their own if the masseuses had extra time for it.

Sophie had spent most of the time signing everybody in, and he had spent his time parking trailers and helping ladies get set up. The two cowboys who were in charge of the horses helped when it was packed with ladies trying to check in and park their vehicles. They were very nice and seemed to be happy to be there, helping. When the last lady checked in, Sophie checked her off the list and relaxed. It was always nice to have everybody arrive.

And now the fun would begin.

* * *

By the time the welcome night dinner party began, Riley had been busy making sure everyone was settled in and had nothing else that needed to be done before it got dark. He had been impressed by all the ladies and their excitement about being at his campground. More than ever, he was determined that he would make this group of ladies happy. Tucker had driven out to support him and to check it out, and he was glad his brother was here. They had discussed the possibility if Riley couldn't be there some weekend, then Tucker would fill in for him.

They stood near the opening of the tent, welcoming the ladies to the party and showing them the food table and pointing out the restrooms. And he thanked everyone for coming, and they thanked him for holding the event.

Maggie, Ida, and Connie were a very nice trio of ladies in their fifties. The group had them surrounded at the moment, excited to be there.

"You nice ladies are obviously enthusiastic campers. Have you been together for a while?" He smiled at them.

"We have been camping together since this group started, about five years ago," Maggie said. "We aren't even from the same area. I'm from the Saint Angelo area, a good six-hour trip. Ida is from Midlothian, Texas, also about six hours away. And Connie is from

Crocket, a small town about five hours away. So we're all approximately the same distance, and a lot of times the drive is similar for us. Sometimes, we meet at a hotel and spend a couple of nights visiting and shopping, just the three of us."

The other two ladies nodded in agreement.

Ida smiled. "We really enjoy having met each other at camp and all the other people, but we connected with a special friendship. We all lost our husbands, oddly at similar times. But we don't think about that much now. We're trying to move on and this group has helped us know that we have to have a new outlook on our life after losing the ones we loved." Ida pushed her hair back and even though there was brief sadness in her eyes, she smiled again. "And it's all because of this big group, but especially the three of us connecting. I'm so grateful for it. And we can tell this is going to be a great weekend, so thank you."

"You're welcome," he said, taken aback by her sincerity.

Connie looked at him seriously. "I agree. We are always thankful to have found this camping group and all the beautiful places we find to camp. And we are very grateful for this new place. It's going to be great. And I can't wait to ride a horse in the morning. Even though I'm from the Crocket area where there are a lot of cowboys, I don't own a horse. But I love to ride when I get the chance. So I totally love you providing the opportunity to ride on the beach."

"Great. I can tell you we were thrilled to offer the McIntyre Ranch's horses to do that. By the way, this is my brother Tucker, and he's here to help with the horse rides tomorrow."

Tucker lifted his hat from his head and smiled. "Glad to meet you, ladies. I feel in my heart that y'all are going to have a great time because Riley here has always been one to work hard to make things good. So I hope you do."

All three of the ladies shook Tucker's hand, and Riley could tell they were pleased that he had another member of his family involved. He was, too.

After they headed inside, Tucker looked at him seriously. "Great group of ladies. I think you are going to have a booked camp after this one because these ladies will put the word out."

"That's kind of what I feel. And also, if I don't please them, then I don't have any business being in this business."

"It won't be because you haven't been trying. You did a great job. When I drove up and saw how packed it was and how this huge tent fits in, it all looks great. And I also crossed paths with Sophie, and she is highly excited."

Riley was relieved to hear that she was still excited. "She is really encouraging."

Tucker grinned. "I agree. And I think a lot of that comes from you."

"In all honesty, I am pretty much hooked on that great lady."

Tucker's grin grew wider. "I suspected you were. That's cool, because, with just the little bit she's said about you and how great a job you've done with this, I suspect she feels the way you do."

Riley hoped so. He hoped more than anything that she was in love with him, because he knew he was in love with Sophie.

CHAPTER SIXTEEN

While the talented musician played in the background, everyone greeted one another and chatted before they gathered their food from the buffet table and sat at the tables.

Sophie stepped up to the microphone at the end of a song. "Welcome, everyone. I am thrilled to get to hang out with you all again, and I'm especially thrilled to be trying out a brand-new camping spot. We lucked out to be the first group to snag the McIntyre Camp, and I've been very impressed with how hard Riley has worked to make it a place you'll enjoy. I'm looking forward to your comments on the paper you'll be given before you leave. If you don't mind filling it out, it will help our wonderful host, who I think has done an outstanding job.

"Anyway, we're going to have a delicious meal and visiting time tonight. Tomorrow is going to be a fantastic day. The great addition is you can ride a horse along the beach. And I love getting spoiled with the massages, facials, and manicures we have on our trips. And then, of course, the beach is out there, depending on how cold you like it—it is an early time of the year. I took my shoes off yesterday and walked in the water, and I think I can swim in it. If not, just sitting in a chair in the sunshine talking with y'all will be wonderful too. So y'all come see me because I've missed all of you. Let's have a great weekend, ladies. Now, officially meet Riley McIntyre."

Everyone's excitement was heard in their clapping as she walked from the microphone and gave the spot to Riley. He smiled warmly at her as they passed on the two steps to the stage.

"You did a great job," he said to her, then he stepped to the mic. "Hi, everyone. Sophie is a great camp organizer. She has helped me get this first group camp in order, and I am really grateful to her and very thrilled to welcome each of you. I'm going to get off the stage so you can eat and visit. But if you think of something I should add to my camp, I would appreciate your comments. If you have a problem that needs attention, let me know so it can be fixed. We want it to be the best for you. Anyway, thank you. Have a great time, and I am so happy to have y'all here as my first group of glampers."

Sophie watched with delight as Riley stepped off the platform to a burst of loud cheers and clapping. His expression was pleased, and she was happy to be here and see it.

"I don't know if you can tell they are excited and really glad to be here, but they are," she said when he reached her.

"I'm really thankful to know. Now, if I can just make sure they get the treatment and everything that they deserve."

She patted his arm. "I have no doubt you will."

"Well, thank you very much. All right, go have dinner with all your ladies. Tucker and I are going to get us something to eat and sit outside at one of the campfires out front and visit. If you need us, you'll know where we'll be. I don't want to get in the way of y'all having a great time."

"Thank you. You two have a good time." She watched him walk to the back, and then he and Tucker headed for the food. He had done such a good job.

She could tell just by looking at the excitement on everyone's faces, they were glad to test out a new place.

And she was glad to be here more than any camp she'd ever been to. It was going to be a great weekend.

* * *

He and Tucker sat down in two wooden chairs at the fire pit and placed their glasses of tea on the small log table between them.

"This has been really interesting," Tucker said. "I think you've started something really cool."

Relief had washed over Riley ever since being inside and he'd felt the excitement in the room.

"Thanks. I get a positive feeling from all of them."

"I do too. And I think it's going to be fun. I'm thinking you can do something like this for couples, too."

"Yeah, maybe so. The two weeks of regular camp for couples or families were great. But checking into adding extra stuff could work out. But I'm not sure I'd want to do four solid weeks of what's coming tomorrow and Sunday." He was serious. He'd need to compare the two camps later.

An hour later, they were still sitting there, listening to the music inside and talking. The ladies had not come out of the building yet and with the delightful sounds of laughter, it was clear they were having a good time.

"The sound of them enjoying themselves makes me happy."

"I see why. They are having a blast."

He did hope that he got to talk to Sophie again before the night was over, to get her feelings on the way the evening went. And also to see whether there was anything else he needed to do tomorrow to make sure it was right. He wasn't out here hiding; anyone who wanted to find him could walk out the door and see him. But nobody had walked out that opening yet.

"I think they're having a good time. Whether it's because of the food, the singing, or just them being so happy to see each other, I don't know. But I'm hoping I know something tonight before Sophie turns in for the night."

Tucker laughed and looked at him as if he were crazy. "Come on, brother. You know good and well you're going to see her before you go to bed. Are you never taking that next step?"

"Not this weekend. We're trying to keep everything quiet during this camp because it's about her group. But, in all honesty, I love her. So, like I said, this weekend, we're just keeping our relationship quiet because we want the opinion about the camp, not what they think about me and Sophie. I would appreciate it if you didn't say anything."

"I won't. I'll be back out tomorrow and help you with the horse rides and I'm going to stay out of your way. Who knows—you two may sneak some time together."

Riley shook his head. "No, we're not going to do that. I mean, if she comes out of there later and I'm not around here, I hope I see her at my camper's fire pit. Her tiny trailer is pretty close to mine. We did that in case we needed to discuss anything about camp."

Tucker stared at him with a disbelieving expression. "Come on, dude—you did that so you could see her before she went to bed at night. I'm going to head back to the ranch, but call if you need me."

"All right. Thanks for coming out tonight. I'm thinking positive and tomorrow will be a great day. But it's great for you to watch the opening, the middle and the end in case I need you to handle the event for me sometime."

"I'd be glad to do it, but hope you ever needing me isn't because of something bad happening. If you want to go off and enjoy a weekend, I'll fill in for you."

Riley watched his brother head to the parking area, relieved that Tucker had been here tonight. He looked at his watch and realized it was actually later than he thought; he headed over to the beach café to make sure they'd gotten closed up on time. They had, so he strode around and double-checked all the campfires, and then headed back over and looked in the tent's entrance.

They were in groups, laughing and talking. It was obvious that these ladies enjoyed themselves. A few were even out on the dance floor in groups, talking, dancing, and having a good time. He glimpsed Sophie, surrounded by a gaggle of ladies talking to her. He understood why they stood around her, talking to her— because there was nothing he wanted to do more at that moment.

She was beautiful.

He backed away from the opening and headed to the back side of the tent, where he knew the food crew was loading things up. He made sure everything was good with them and they thanked him for a good evening. He thanked them for being there and then headed off to let them finish packing and head out.

As far as he could tell—until he talked to Sophie—their first night as a glamping camp was a success. But talking to Sophie before he could clarify that was still a priority.

Or maybe he just wanted to talk to Sophie. He was definitely looking forward to it.

* * *

It was nearly midnight when Sophie watched the last campers head off to bed. She had wanted more than anything, all night long, to go find Riley and tell him how much fun everyone was having. And how much everyone was looking forward to what was planned for tomorrow. But she hadn't; she'd tell him as soon as she left the building and headed to her camper, if she could find him. She looked around the enormous tent to make sure it was still neat, since the waitresses had cleaned up before they left at ten o'clock. All of her campers knew that hanging out after the workers left meant they'd have to help keep things cleaned up, and they'd done a fairly good job.

She picked up a couple of forgotten, empty glasses and tossed them in the garbage, and then she headed to her camper, hoping Riley was waiting at his fire pit. Her heart rolled to life when she turned the corner and saw the fire burning softly in front of his camper.

He sat in the chair, and she walked in his direction.

He stood up, smiling. "Hey there. Did you have a good evening?"

She did, but seeing him now made it even better. "Riley, everyone had a wonderful time. Not just because they haven't seen each other in several months, but everyone loved the look of this beautiful camp. They liked you and can't wait until tomorrow. Everyone is excited and talking about riding a horse on the beach. So I wanted you to know your idea is phenomenal."

"That is what I needed to hear. I'm really glad everyone is looking forward to it. And with the two guys who are running the ride and Tucker helping them, that will free me up to make sure everything else is running well. It looks like we might be on a good trial run here to make this a success for your friends."

She wanted so much to hug him and kiss him. But

they'd agreed none of that right now, so instead she sank down in the chair closest to his, and he sank down in his. There was some space in between them, which she knew he had done on purpose so no one would think that they were a couple.

"I want you to know that I wanted to come out several times and look for you and tell you what people were saying. But in all honesty, I was afraid if I came out and started talking to you, I'd have trouble going back in, where I needed to be."

He smiled and his gaze dropped to her lips, then back up to her eyes. "You just made my day. Because I had to sneak by there once to look in and get a vision of you having a great time. I was happy for you but knowing you were tempted to come find me thrills me."

"And that thrills me." She chuckled, because this information was wonderful.

"I was hoping I would see you before you went to bed. I promise I won't keep you up too much later." He put his elbows on his knees, which brought them closer. "And I'm really fighting off wanting to kiss you, but it just takes one person spotting us, so I'm going to hold back."

She smiled and leaned her elbows on her knees, so tempted she could barely stay back.

He stood. "I think you need to head on to bed. Let's have a great day tomorrow."

Sophie rose, knowing he was right. "I don't think there's anything that can stop it from being a great day. Sleep good." She smiled, then headed across the short distance to her camper. She didn't look back as she opened the door and walked inside.

She looked out the corner of her window and saw he'd sank back into his chair and dropped his forehead into his palm. She felt bad at how happy she was to know his night was going to be as hard as hers.

CHAPTER SEVENTEEN

"That was really good, Sophie," Maggie said as they finished up their morning exercise class. Everyone but the three friends had already headed to get breakfast.

"I'm glad you enjoyed it," Sophie said. It was actually a stretching class; they really didn't exercise hard, just got out there together to stretch, move their arms and bend their legs, and breathed deeply to help themselves get ready for a beautiful day. "I was hoping y'all would enjoy it. It's been a little while since we've done that."

"Yes, it has been," Connie said. "But we've got more on the way now, with the warm spring starting us off on the right track. I'm going riding today—first time I've gotten to do that in a long time, and I am excited."

"Me too," Ida agreed.

Sophie loved their excitement. "I am so glad y'all are among everyone really looking forward to it."

Maggie studied her. "I have a question about that gorgeous cowboy Riley running the camp. Are you two interested in each other? I could have sworn that I caught y'all looking at each other a few times at the beginning of the gathering last night. I kept watching, but then he went outside with his brother and you hung out with us, so I'm just curious if you're interested in him. I would be chasing him, if I were you."

The other two studied her, wondering as well.

"Well...I have to agree that he is a very handsome man, and he started a wonderful camp. Right now, our concentration is on helping get a great camp going here."

Ida frowned. "Now, honey, just because you're working on this camp doesn't mean you can't work on him. I mean, you are a lot younger than we are and never married and don't date. I am just curious when you think you're going to."

She sighed. "I'll have to say, I could start with Riley. He is an awesome man, and he feels the same way, but we're concentrating on the camp this weekend. I appreciate y'all's concern."

They all stared at her with understanding, then they each gave her a hug and basically told her they understood but she shouldn't pass this up.

She watched as they headed back to change out of their cute little workout outfits. She took a deep breath and was very thankful everybody else had already walked off before they started that conversation.

She had seen Riley when she'd headed across the camp to teach this early class on the beach. He had looked very busy talking to the cowboys over by the horses. Now, as she headed toward the breakfast at the outdoor restaurant, she was pleased to see all the smiles of the ladies this morning. Instead of sitting at a table she went to the counter and ordered one of the already cooked egg and sausage tacos and a cup of coffee. After she'd paid and they'd handed it to her, she walked over to one of the fire pits. It wasn't lit up at the moment, but she sank down in a chair and took a sip of coffee before setting it on the log side table, then took a bite of her breakfast taco. From where she sat, she could see the horse area and saw Riley, Tucker, and the other two cowboys getting all the horses saddled.

She smiled, watching them. The ladies were going to love their rides. She knew it was Tucker and his ranch hands who were going to go out on the rides. Riley had said he would go if he had time, but she liked how he was looking to make sure everything was correct even if he didn't get to go. He also had to make sure that the masseuse and manicurist had everything they needed. That was why he had two men from the ranch and Tucker also to oversee the riding.

She finished her breakfast taco and her coffee; then she headed back to her trailer to change out of her workout set into shorts and a tank top with a bathing suit underneath, just in case she decided she wanted to lie in a beach lounger and enjoy some sunshine. When she came out of her camper, Riley stood by the fire pit.

"Hi there," she said as she walked across the short distance.

At the sound of her words, he'd spun toward her. "Hello." He smiled, his eyes sparkling.

She wanted to throw her arms around him, but refrained. "Are you going horseback riding this morning?"

"I'd like to, but I have too many things to make sure are going right. But Tucker and the fellas are about ready for the first ride of the day. It should be fun for them. I hope the ladies are looking forward to it."

"Believe me, they are. Especially three of them."

He grinned. "The ones who kept you out by the water talking so long after you led them all in stretches?"

She laughed. "You saw. Yes, them."

"I was walking to the horse pen and saw the four of you in deep conversation. They're really nice ladies. They asked me last night if I was interested in you, because they thought we would make a great couple."

Sophie's mouth fell open for a moment. "They didn't pressure you, did they? Because they were asking me the same thing this morning. I had to be honest with them, so I told them we were concentrating on their camp this weekend but who knows…we could end up dating."

He grinned. "That's kind of what I told them, too. Maybe not in those words, but similar."

"I think we are really on the same target." She could not let go of his eyes. "I better meet the ladies I'm getting my manicure done with this morning."

"Good idea. I went earlier and made sure all the doors were open and rooms were ready. As I was leaving, the workers were arriving. Have a good time. If there's something I've missed or that I need to work on, let me know."

"You're doing a great job." She headed off, feeling his eyes following her. She wanted so badly to run back and fall into his arms and maybe steal a kiss from him, but she didn't. Instead, she forced her feet to keep walking just in case somebody was watching.

* * *

By two o'clock, Riley decided to go on the upcoming

horse ride because he didn't seem to have anything that needed his attention right now. All the ladies going in and out of the tents where they were getting facials, manicures, and massages were having a great time, if their laughing and smiling was any indication. He'd spotted Sophie several times, and she was having a blast. She saw him once and waved; then her expression told him she realized she hadn't planned to wave at him. That she did made him happy and helped him hold out and not expose his feelings for her. Riding a horse was an excellent distraction. Plus, he needed to feel what his campers were feeling so he could improve it if he saw a need.

The ride was still thirty minutes away, so he walked out toward the beach. He needed to check on how everyone was doing, make sure everybody was enjoying themselves, and that they were safe. He had hired a lifeguard, who was sitting in the lifeguard chair, to keep the swimmers safe.

"Everything going okay?" He looked up at John, who was around twenty but worked as a lifeguard on weekends.

188

"So far, so good. They aren't swimming really, but standing in the water, having conversations. These ladies love to visit."

Riley chuckled. "Yes, they do. This is their first camping trip of the summer, so they're catching up on their time away from each other. Thanks for watching them."

He headed toward the two high school girls who were bringing orders out from the food bar and thanked them for the good job they were doing taking care of the ladies.

He had thought the ladies might enjoy being waited on out by the ocean, and it appeared he'd been right.

Finally, he headed back to the horse pen and let the guys know he was going to ride this time. He had on his long shorts, tennis shoes, and t-shirt instead of being dressed up like a cowboy but he could still ride a horse.

Abe grinned at him. He and Kurt were dressed like they dressed working on the ranch: in jeans, t-shirts, and boots, and topped off with their cowboy hats.

"You can ride them any way you want. My legs are so white under these jeans that I'd be burned to a crisp."

"I totally would too, but I wore shorts over the last month while I worked so I'd be prepared."

"Good idea," Kurt said as he walked by, leading a horse, and tied it to the fence.

Tucker laughed. "Yeah, us cowboys get used to a different attire on the beach than most people. But this has been a great day, Riley. The women have really enjoyed it."

"I'm glad. And that's why I'm going on a ride, so I can see just how wonderful it is to them."

Abe and Kurt went to work, getting the horses gathered up and tied at the fence to wait on their riders.

Tucker looked at him. "If you don't need me on this ride, then I'll head on to the ranch. But if you need me, I'll stay."

"No, head on out. They can take care of the horses when we get back."

"Okay, but I'll be out here first thing in the morning to help with rides, and then I'll help them load the horses up and take them back to the ranch."

"Sounds good."

Riley walked to the fence with his brother. "Thanks for all your assistance. You've been an immense help to me. I overheard some ladies who had gone on a horse ride with you. You were a hit. Some of them were around Sophie's age, so there is some potential there."

Tucker's eyebrows dipped together. "I'm not looking for a date, especially from a group of gals who could live hours away."

"Fine, have it your way." Riley laughed as Tucker lifted his hand and headed toward his truck.

Riley turned back around just as he saw Sophie walk up to the fence with a couple of ladies. It looked as if she were going for a horse ride too. He had already committed to taking his brother's place, so it looked like they'd be going on a ride together. He walked over and began helping tighten the saddles and making sure the horses were ready for the ride.

Sophie walked over to him. "Are you riding with us?"

He glanced over the fence and grinned. "I am.

191

Looks like we're going to have a good group on this ride."

Her eyes twinkled at him. "Yes, we are. I waited until now because I thought since it was a hotter time of day fewer ladies would ride and I wouldn't be taking up a horse earlier. I was wrong—it looks like all twenty of the horses are going to be ridden."

"That was my thought too. And Tucker decided to head on home and come back to help tomorrow."

"Great." She grinned, then looked at the ladies. "Everybody, if you get any ideas you want to share with Riley, remember to do it. He is coming on this ride with us to get a firsthand feeling of our experience. So help him out if you think of something that will improve this fantastic weekend. You can leave him a note before you leave tomorrow. He's counting on those notes to help him make it even better in hopes we'll want to come back next year."

One lady frowned. "I've loved all of it so far. It's been delightful."

"I am thankful for that. Guys, are we ready to ride?" Riley asked the cowboys.

Abe nodded. "Ladies, we'll assist you in getting in the saddle, so wait on one of us."

Within a few minutes, everyone was loaded, and they followed Kurt out the gate. Abe rode along the side of everyone, and Riley took the end of the line. Everyone was smiling as they rode past him, and then he fell in line behind them. He was smiling too, even bigger when he saw Sophie look over her shoulder and smile back at him.

* * *

The ocean ride was so fun. Something Sophie had never done but hoped to do again. The horses even enjoyed it as they walked casually along the water in the sand and through the water as it would roll in and cover their hooves sometimes.

She had been riding a few horses ahead of Riley as he rode in the back, keeping everyone in his eyesight, probably in case he saw someone needing help. Maggie, Ida, and Connie all looked over their shoulders at her and grinned several times. She knew they were loving the ride but also had noticed she had dropped back, and they were urging her to drop back and ride beside Riley.

And why not? She looked over her shoulder at Riley. "Your horse riding on the beach is a tremendous success."

He sped his horse up and moved to ride beside her. "I am very glad to hear that. And I've been wanting to ride beside you since we got on horseback. You know, to talk about the success of the camp." He grinned at her.

"Me too." She grinned back at him. "This entire trip has been fun. You've done great. And the meal tonight will be a hit and another fun night of visiting together. I guarantee you that everybody will look forward to coming back next year. Everybody will hate to leave tomorrow afternoon. Me especially," she whispered. And she meant it.

"I'm going to dread you leaving, too. But believe me, we will see each other. I'll have to drive wherever you are working during the week and take you out to dinner. And some weekends when I'm having camp, you may have to drive up and see me. Or I'll have to get the guys to run a regular camp for me while I come see you. Sounds complicated, but we'll get it figured out—don't worry about that."

He spoke so that she was the only one who could hear him, and it slammed into her how much she didn't want to drive away.

Someone yelled, "Dolphin!" and they looked in the direction being pointed at to see several dolphins swimming in the waves, as if keeping up with them. It was a magnificent view, and all the ladies loved it, riding their horses and watching three dolphins swimming offshore beside them. It was fun to watch; she loved it.

But when she glanced back at Riley, she suddenly knew without a doubt that she loved him more than anything. And there was no denying it.

None.

For the first time in her life, she loved a man with all her heart.

CHAPTER EIGHTEEN

Alice drove into Seth's driveway Sunday afternoon. She had been working the front desk at the inn today but had gotten one of the other ladies to take over for her so she could take a break and check on him. She had called him several times, and he hadn't answered, and he always answered her calls. She went into the kitchen and told Lisa and Zane where she was going and why. Zane and Seth had become friends since they'd met at the inn; they didn't live far from each other and they got along really well.

"If you need me, call me," he said. "But there may be nothing wrong. He was going to work on his gutters, I think."

"Yes, he was," Alice agreed.

Lisa waved her on. "Go, and call us if you need us. Or just call and let us know he's okay."

"I will. Thanks." With that, she got into her car.

Now, she pulled into his driveway. She quickly climbed from her car, hurried to the front door and knocked. When there was no answer, she knocked harder and then called his name. Still no answer. She spun around and hurried to the back of the house. She almost passed out when she saw Seth on the ground, with the ladder lying on top of him.

"Seth!" She raced to him. He wasn't conscious. How long had he been out? She had been calling for at least twenty minutes. "Honey, wake up! Can you not hear me?"

She spotted a bump on his forehead as she whipped her phone out of her jean pocket and quickly dialed 911. This was not normal. She carefully eased the ladder off him and then sank to the ground, urging him to wake up. She rubbed his sweet forehead and kissed his cheek, and knew she had to see him wake up again. Just as she heard the sirens coming down the road, he slowly opened his eyes.

"What happened?"

Tears rolled out of her eyes as she cupped his face with her hands. "You must have fallen off your ladder, and it fell on top of you. Which doesn't sound like you at all, so something had to have caused the accident. The ambulance just pulled into the driveway so they'll be back here in a minute."

He didn't say anything more, but nodded and closed his eyes again.

Her heart rammed against her chest as she stared into his face. He had to be okay. She bent down and kissed his forehead again, then looked up and saw the men bringing the stretcher around the house.

"I'm so glad y'all are here. He woke up briefly just now and asked what happened, then he closed his eyes again. I moved the ladder, but it was on top of him."

The guys told her they would take care of him, and she moved out of their way on weak legs. He didn't wake up as they checked him out and then loaded him into the ambulance. They headed for the hospital, with her following.

She called Jackson and told him what was going on so he could tell the others, and he said they would come to the hospital. Then she called Lisa and told her so they'd know and could take care of everything at the inn. She didn't talk long because she couldn't; all she could think about was the man she loved. She prayed he wasn't as hurt as it seemed. She prayed he wasn't about to die—leave her like William had when he'd died.

By the time she pulled into the emergency room parking lot, grabbed her purse, and ran to the ambulance, they were pushing him inside.

The driver glanced over his shoulder at her. "If you could fill in his information at the emergency desk as much as you can, that would be good. Wait in the waiting room, then they'll come out and let you know how he's doing."

"Yes, okay," she said, noticing Seth was still not moving. She hurried to the desk and told the lady his name, age, and that he lived in town but she didn't have his insurance information. If it wasn't in his back pocket, she could send someone to his house to get it, but she wasn't leaving him right now.

"How are you related to him?" the lady asked.

She wanted to say fiancée or wife, but she wasn't either because she hadn't encouraged him to ask her yet. Even though she knew he wanted to. "I'm his girlfriend, but soon-to-be fiancée."

"You own the restaurant, the Star Gazer Inn, right?"

"Umm, yes, I'm Alice McIntyre."

"It's a great place. You can go sit down, and I'll call you when we know something."

She nodded and went to one of the seats. There were other people in the emergency room, but not many. Strange as it was, she didn't know any of them. Suddenly, the door opened and Tucker hurried in. She was shocked to see him because the ranch was a good distance from town and she hadn't expected any of her family to get there yet.

"Mom." He took her into his arms. "I was coming back from camp when I got the call and I was close."

She clung to him. "He's inside and was still

passed out when they rolled him in."

"Any idea what's wrong with him?"

"He fell from the ladder, is what it looked like." She backed up and sat back down, and he sat beside her. "He opened his eyes for a moment and asked me what was wrong. But he passed back out instantly. I'm scared and so glad you're here."

"I'm glad I was close. I know how much you care for him."

"I love him very, very dearly. But obviously he had fallen off the ladder, or something had caused him to fall off the ladder. The ladder was lying on top of him, and he has a big bump on his forehead. I'm praying that it's just something that will go away."

He hugged her. "I'm praying with you, Mom," he said just as Jackson and Nina came in the door, and right behind them was Dallas, Lorna, and Landon.

* * *

Riley and Sophie stood beside each other and waved good-bye to the last campers as they drove away. He had really enjoyed the weekend, but now he looked at Sophie. "The first glamping weekend is over and I had a blast. I hope they did too."

She looked at him as if he were crazy. "Of course they did. Out of all the ones I've held or been to all these years, that was one of the best ever. And I have a feeling you're going to see that when you go looking at their little papers they filled out for you. I never heard even one complaint."

He breathed in a deep breath and let it out slowly. "I hoped that's how it would turn out, but I really wanted to make it the best it can be so you and your group will race back here as soon as possible. Maybe some of them will decide they want to come back on their own and bring their family. But, most of all, you being here made it wonderful."

She leaned her shoulder against his. "Ditto. I loved being here."

Unable to stop himself after all weekend of restraining and knowing they were now the only ones left, he leaned forward and kissed her as he enveloped her in his arms. She wrapped her arms around him and joined in on the kiss.

After a long, deep, emotional kiss, he pulled back and looked into her eyes. "I don't know if you realize this, but this weekend just made me crazier about you."

"I agree. Very much."

He was about to say more when his phone rang. He was tempted to ignore it and kiss her again. But it might be one of the campers who'd just left and now needed help, so he pulled his phone out of his pocket and looked at the screen. It was Jackson, so he clicked Accept and before he could say anything, Jackson spoke.

"I called to let you know that Mom called, and they've taken Seth to the hospital. He had fallen off a ladder and was unconscious when she found him. Anyway, we're all heading up there and wanted you to know in case you wanted to come too. If you can't, I'll keep you informed. She was very upset when she called me."

"I'll be there. The last camper just left. It'll take me a little bit, but I'm on my way."

"Okay. Be careful."

He hung up and stared at Sophie. "Mom's boyfriend, the one we expect she'll marry soon, fell off a ladder and is at the hospital. I need to go up there to be with Mom. If something were to happen to him, that would be really rough on Mom. My brothers are already on their way with their wives, so I've got to go."

"I'll go with you, if you don't mind. I really liked your mom, and I'd hate for something bad to happen."

"That would be great. Is your trailer locked?"

"Yes. I've already got it ready to haul. But do you want me to follow you, or do you want to bring me back here later? I can do whatever you want."

"It's up to you. I mean, you can follow me with it and then you'd be able to leave sooner."

"Are you coming back out here?"

"It's not that far a drive, so I can bring you back."

"Perfect, so I can ride with you. I just need to grab my purse and lock my Jeep."

"Great. I'll turn the truck on while you grab your purse."

He looked relieved to have her ride with him, and

she wanted more than anything to be with him if he needed her.

Moments later, they were on the road, headed toward the hospital on Star Gazer Island.

"So your mom is in love with him?"

"Yes. My dad's been dead now for over three years. She hasn't rushed into this with Seth, but we can all tell she loves him. He's a great man, and it's clear he loves her and is just giving her all the time she needs. He lost his wife a few years earlier, so he understands what she's been through."

"He sounds like a great man, to give her the time she needs."

"I agree."

When they arrived at the hospital, he took her hand and they walked inside together. His mom was there, along with his brothers and Dallas's wife, Lorna, and Jackson's wife, Nina.

"Mom," he said, noticing everybody still looked worried. "Have you heard anything?"

She stood and walked into his arms, and they hugged. "They just said he's awake. And his memory is coming in and out. He has a concussion. They're getting him into a room and then I'll be able to go in and see him."

He had glanced at his brothers and they were all nodding.

Tucker was the first to speak. "They just came out and told her that, but said it wouldn't take long to come get her. We'll know what waiting area to move to when they come out. And we'll hopefully know how bad his concussion is. Obviously when that ladder fell on him, it slammed into him really hard."

His mom reached out a hand for Sophie. "Thank you for coming."

"We had just waved the last camper good-bye when he got the call. I hate this has happened, but I am so glad I hadn't left so that I could come be with y'all." Sophie leaned in and hugged his mom.

"Thank you very much," his mom said, as she hugged Sophie too.

He watched the two most important women in his life hugging, and he knew without a doubt he was going to find out how much he meant to Sophie. But first he needed to make sure Seth was okay, which would mean his mom would be okay.

CHAPTER NINETEEN

After Alice was able to go in and see Seth, the group all looked at one another.

"Mom was truly scared he was in danger of dying, I think," Riley said.

Jackson shook his head slightly. "I never thought I would say this, but she needs to get married. She loves Seth—it's obvious. I think she just put it off because she was opening the inn, but you can tell they love each other. And Dad would want what was best for her. He would want her to have love if she met the right man. And I believe she has, don't y'all agree?"

All the brothers agreed and discussed encouraging their mother to marry Seth.

Sophie watched them but glanced at Nina when she stood suddenly.

She put her fingers over her lips and suddenly swallowed. "I'm going to the bathroom." She hurried toward the restroom.

"Are you okay?" Jackson called.

"Yes," she said, but she didn't sound so good.

Lorna had taken the baby outside to walk around a bit with him, so Sophie was not going to leave Nina in the bathroom alone after seeing the look on her face. "I think I'm going to take a break in the restroom, too. I'll be right back." She headed down the hall. When she entered the restroom, she heard what she thought she would hear: Nina in the bathroom stall, throwing up. She went to the sink and grabbed some paper towels, wet them, and wrung them out. Then she walked to the bathroom door and held them underneath. "Nina, here's some wet paper towels."

Nina took them. "Thank you. I may be getting something. I just suddenly had to, uh…" Her voice disappeared as she threw up again.

"Have you eaten anything that would make you

throw up or been around anybody who would make you sick?"

"I don't think so," she said, her voice weak.

Sophie asked the question she suspected was the reason for the nausea. "Do you think you could be pregnant?"

"I'm trying not to get too hopeful, because I've been having trouble getting pregnant, but I'm praying that's what this is. It's worth this throwing up."

"Do you think you're finished? I'll help you come out of there and let you rinse your mouth out."

"I think it's better." The door opened and Nina stepped out of the stall. "I can walk, but thank you."

They crossed to the sinks and Sophie studied the paleness of Nina's skin. She'd had a friend once who had a similar situation when she learned she was pregnant.

Nina turned on the water and rinsed her mouth out.

Sophie held more paper towels out to her.

She smiled as she took them and dried her face. "I have to get a test."

"There might be one down in the hospital store. I'll go down there and check. Since we're right by the elevators, it shouldn't take long to look."

"Could you, please? I'm feeling better, so I'll go out there. I'll watch for you. If I'm not pregnant, I don't want to tell Jackson right now."

"I'll come right back."

They split up outside the door. Nina would tell the guys that Sophie had gone to the store for some gum. Sophie was relieved to find two different pregnancy tests at the store and bought both. She tucked the tests into her purse and when she stepped off the elevator, Nina saw her; she said something to the guys and came her way.

"I told them we were going to find Lorna and the baby."

They headed straight to the bathroom. "They had two tests so I got both of them for you so you can double test." She held the tests out to Nina.

"Thank you." Nina took the boxes and entered the restroom stall. Within moments, she cried out, "Both tests say I'm having a baby."

The joy in her voice was highly apparent and Sophie understood why. This made her remember how much she'd once wanted marriage and babies, too. "I'm so excited. And I know there's a man out there who will be just as excited."

Smiling, Nina came out of the restroom, holding both of the tests. "He's going to be so happy. Let's go so I can make his day."

They went outside and Sophie saw that Lorna and the baby were back, and Dallas had his arm around her. Perfect; they were all here.

Nina walked straight up to her husband. "This is kind of a weird day to be saying this since we're worried about Seth and your mom, but…Jackson, we're expecting a baby." She held both tests out for Jackson to see.

He yelped for joy and pulled her into his arms, lifting her feet off the ground. "I'm so happy." Then he kissed her as they twirled on the floor.

All his brothers clapped him on the shoulder, congratulating him.

Riley moved to Sophie's side. "You suspected

that, didn't you?"

She leaned her head against his shoulder. "Yes, after I got in there and asked her a few questions. I went downstairs and bought the tests. She was so thrilled."

He patted her arm. "You're awesome."

Their mother walked out of Seth's room, which was just down the hall. She was smiling. "He's going to be okay. He has a concussion, but it's not horrible, and he knew who I was, so that was wonderful. I'm going to stay here with him, but you can go on home. I told him y'all were out here but he's now sleeping again, coming in and out..." She paused and looked around at everyone. "Is something wrong?"

"We're thrilled Seth is going to be okay." Jackson was still holding Nina. "We have some news we just found out. We're expecting our first baby. We just found out after Nina tested two times in the restroom."

"Oh, my goodness!" Alice moved toward them. "Come in here—I've got to give you a hug. I'm so excited." They embraced her and all three of their faces beamed with smiles.

* * *

Riley looked over at Sophie as he drove them back toward the camp. "This was a great day. Thank you for going with me to see about Mom and Seth. I'm so glad he's going to be okay. And then for helping Nina learn their joyous news. They had been trying for a baby and I think they were worried they weren't going to have one. Jackson had told me he worried that she was getting really stressed out about not being able to have babies or him not being able to have babies, even though they'd been trying for a few months. But now they can rest easy."

"She's ecstatic, and so was he. You have a great family. And though I haven't met Seth, he must be a great man if your mother loves him so much."

"Thank you. I love my family and I'm glad you like them." His mom and brothers and sisters-in-law had nothing but good things to say about Sophie, and he couldn't think of a negative thing, either.

When they got back to the camp, they got out and walked over to her Jeep. She unlocked the door, and he opened it for her. She turned toward him, and he wanted to keep her here. He slipped his arms around her and pulled her into his arms.

"Thank you for going with me. My family totally appreciated it."

"I'm glad I hadn't left yet. I'm so glad everything went well."

He bent down and gently touched her lips with his and she responded instantly, which sent thrills running through him. The kiss increased in depth and longing before they finally pulled away. "You call me when you get home. Or, on the way. Call me whenever you want to."

She nodded. "I will." She slid into the seat and he closed the door.

It took everything in him not to yank the door open and pull her back to him. But he forced himself to step back and watch her leave. He wanted to chase after her more than anything else in his life.

Nothing had changed by the next morning when he woke up. A few minutes later, he strode into the barn at the main house, where they all tried to meet for coffee every morning before work. Dallas wasn't there because he was busy at his ranch, getting ready for a sale he was having in a few days. But Jackson and Tucker were drinking their coffee, watching him as he walked in.

"Cup of coffee?" Jackson asked.

"A huge, strong cup, please." He raked a hand through his hair after he had removed his hat. He sank into a chair. "I had a really rough night."

"So what do you feel so horrible about?" Tucker stared at him seriously as Jackson quickly filled a cup.

He turned and handed the coffee to him. "Have anything to do with Sophie?"

"I am totally, madly in love with Sophie. I haven't been able to think straight since she left yesterday. And I'm not real sure what to do about it. I mean, sure, we met close to a year ago but we've really only gotten to know each other this month. Not very long. But I've been miserable since she drove off." He took a sip of hot coffee.

Jackson looked at Tucker and then back at him. "Go after her," Jackson said. "Don't let her get away.

If you have feelings, then go tell her. If she doesn't feel the same way or things are moving too fast, she'll tell you."

Tucker cocked his head, looking at him. "I think she feels the same way about you as you do about her. I watched you two a lot over the weekend and though she tried to hide it from all the ladies, I saw it. Get in your truck and go see her. You're not the kind of man who would let a dream escape. Look how you went after that campground that she brought into your thoughts and then it brought her back into your life. Sounds pretty good to me...seems like a plan to me."

"And I agree." Jackson grinned.

Their support was very helpful. "Y'all are right. I've been thinking if I ran after her, it would be too fast. That I might run her off instead. But I can already tell you, if I don't do something pretty quickly then I'm probably going to go crazy. Thanks."

He stood, set his coffee cup down, and then walked out the door.

CHAPTER TWENTY

Alice hadn't been to work in two days because she had been at the hospital with Seth. Thank goodness his memory was back and he was going to get to go home. She had totally committed to remaining with him and making sure he continued to progress over the next few days. And she would come with him for the checkup in three days.

She was looking out the window as the bathroom door opened, and she turned to look at Seth as he came out. He was dressed and ready to go home, wearing the clothes that Lisa had brought from his house. Alice had changed into the jeans and shirt Lisa had picked up from her room at the inn.

Alice walked toward him. "I'm so glad to see you looking like you're actually ready to go home."

He pulled her into his arms and looked into her eyes. "Still some recovery to go but glad the doc says I can do that at home…if I don't climb the ladder right now." He smiled. "The idea that you're going home with me for a few days makes everything all worth it."

Her heart lunged forward and pounded joyously inside her. "I am not thrilled that you got hurt, but it knocked me into reality. Seth, I loved William so very much. And after losing him, you know, it put me on hold for nearly two years until I finally knew I had to make some changes and bought the inn. And then you walked into my life. I knew when I first met you that you were special, and I knew within months that I loved you, but I wasn't ready to love someone yet. I used the inn opening as an excuse and let my still hurting heart fear marrying someone again. It was the fear that I could lose someone else. But you know my fear has been easing up, but not fast enough—until finding you lying on the ground with that ladder on top of you. I knew instantly that if you had died, I'd regret not having married you and sharing love with you for the rest of my life. I love you, Seth, and I don't want to ever lose you. If you still want to marry me, I would marry you this instant." Tears had filled her eyes, she was so full of love and hope.

"I hope my memory is not playing crazy games on me and that I still remember this in an hour. If I forget, then remind me, because I would marry you right now if we could. I hope you really mean what you just said because you just made my future."

Her heart was ecstatic as she lifted her lips to his. They kissed in love and agreement.

She pulled back after a moment. "I know we can't really get married today, but while we're at your house waiting for you to get your brain completely back, we're going to set a date. How does that sound?"

"Wonderful. The sooner, the better. I've was truly blessed that you walked into my life. And we both understand we loved our prior husband and wife, but that doesn't change our love for each other. It just means our lives were blessed with love twice. I love you desperately, and I thank God for you."

She nodded as tears slipped down her cheeks. "I totally agree, my love."

CHAPTER TWENTY-ONE

Riley forced himself to go out to the camp after he'd talked to his brothers. He'd worked on things he needed to get ready for the coming weekend. He had been totally heading toward Corpus Christi when he'd walked out of the barn yesterday morning, but he'd decided to come here and let his brain think what his next move would be. He'd slept in his trailer last night and dreamed of a life with her. He couldn't drop it.

He did not let himself call immediately when he woke up, but at nine, he called. "Sophie, good morning," he said, trying to get his nerves under control.

"Riley, I'm so glad to hear your voice. I haven't been able to get you off my mind since I drove away. I miss you."

Relief swamped him, because he had never heard better words. "And I miss you desperately. I forced myself not to call you yesterday, but to give you another day. I know you have a busy schedule, but is there any way you can come down to the camp today? If you can't, I'll come up there because I have to see you."

"I'll put off going out for an appraisal today and will head your way in a few moments. I can't help myself. Thankfully, I forced myself to do the paperwork I needed to do on a previous one yesterday. So get ready because I'm headed that way and I'll bring an overnight bag if I need to stay."

"You have made me the happiest man alive. Come here to the camp and I'll have lunch ready for us. Drive safe. I love you."

"I love you too."

Emotion swamped him. "Best words I've ever heard."

* * *

Sophie had almost screamed with joy when Riley had called her. She loved him so much, and after she left the hospital, she knew she didn't want to be away from him.

Ever.

She drove through town and headed out toward where the campground was. The closer she got, the more her heart pounded, rising up with joy at getting to see him again. Finally, she drove through the entrance of the campground and was thrilled to see Riley at the door of the office. He was smiling in an ecstatic way as he strode to the Jeep. She was already out the door and slammed it behind her just before he swept her into his arms and covered her lips with a kiss.

She loved him. Loved him desperately.

Hope rallied through her as he deepened the kiss, tightened his hug as though he would never let her go. Then, slowly, he let her feet sink to the ground; his hands came up and cupped her face and he looked into her eyes.

"I'm so glad to see you." He took a deep breath. "I have lunch ready, out near one of the picnic tables on the way to the beach." He took her hand.

"The waves sound wonderful," she said. "But anything with you sounds wonderful. Away from you has become sad and boring." It was true.

His hand tightened on hers as they walked toward the beach. "I guess that should make me sad for you, but it gives me hope and sends thrills through me."

When they walked out onto the sand he headed straight toward a table that had a tablecloth on it and a good-sized basket with a cloth over it. Beside it was a bucket with what looked like a bottle of champagne sticking up out of the ice.

She halted and looked at him.

Riley's lips curled gently into a smile as he lifted his right hand and gently placed his fingertips on her cheek. "I have a question to ask you."

She froze, barely able to breathe.

He let his finger drift from her jaw and reached into the picnic basket. He pulled out a small, black ring box. An emotional gasp escaped her the same instant he dropped to one knee and lifted the top of the ring box.

"Sophie, I love you with all of my heart. You might turn me down, but I must ask if you would marry me and make me the luckiest man in the world. If you need longer, I will court you, date you as long as I need to, but I would rather marry you as soon as possible."

She hadn't said anything because she couldn't; her voice had disappeared. A tear ran down her face; she saw his eyes flare with worry at her silence and her tears, and then, thank goodness, her voice came. "Yes. Marrying you is my dream. I love you so much."

He slid the ring onto her finger. It was a beautiful round diamond engagement ring that she loved almost like she loved him. He pulled her into his arms and kissed her again with so much feeling her knees weakened and she clung happily to to him.

Clung to him like she would for the rest of their lives.

She knew that her life had just changed in the most wonderful way. Not only with the man of her dreams, but a family she cared about as well. But the most important part was Riley.

He was the love she'd been hoping for and waiting for all of her life…and he was well worth the wait.

Coming later in the year!

Sign up for my newsletter for notification:

debraclopton.com/contest

WHAT A HEART'S DESIRE IS MADE OF

Star Gazer Inn of Corpus Christi Bay, Book Four

Starting over time is here and Alice McIntyre is about to take that step as her family and friends attend her wedding to Seth. Life is beginning a new on Star Gazer Island and you are invited to attend!

Meanwhile, Alice's son Tucker has poured himself into the ranch after losing the love of his life several years ago. He's watched his mother start over after losing his dad, and he's watched his brothers find love and happiness. But can he? And then she walks in and sets his world to spinning.

Lisa has found satisfaction being the chef at Star Gazer Inn and is so happy for her friend Alice's newfound love. Lisa is fighting to deny that she also wants to find love to replace her bad first marriage. But she's hasn't gotten over the pain it caused and is determined keeping her heart safe in the kitchen cooking while avoiding longing for love. The only problem is she hired chef Zane Tyson to back her up in the kitchen and now she's seeing him in her future despite trying to deny it.

Once again, relax on the Texas coast and enjoy your stay as Alice, her sons, and her friends continue to find love on the South Texas coast with its sparkling topaz water.

You'll want to dip your toes in and stay awhile.

More Books by Debra Clopton

Star Gazer Inn of Corpus Christi Bay
What New Beginnings are Made of (Book 1)
What Dreams are Made of (Book 2)
What Hopes are Made of (Book 3)
What a Heart's Desire is Made of (Book 4)

Sunset Bay Romance
Longing for Forever (Book 1)
Longing for a Hero (Book 2)
Longing for Love (Book 3)
Longing for Ever After (Book 4)
Longing for You (Book 5)
Longing for Us (Book 6)

Texas Brides & Bachelors
Heart of a Cowboy (Book 1)
Trust of a Cowboy (Book 2)
True Love of a Cowboy (Book 3)

New Horizon Ranch Series
Her Texas Cowboy: Cliff (Book 1)
Rescued by Her Cowboy: Rafe (Book 2)
Protected by Her Cowboy: Chase (Book 3)
Loving Her Best Friend Cowboy: Ty (Book 4)
Family for a Cowboy: Dalton (Book 5)
The Mission of Her Cowboy: Treb (Book 6)
Maddie's Secret Baby (Book 7)
This Cowgirl Loves This Cowboy: Austin (Book 8)

Turner Creek Ranch Series
Treasure Me, Cowboy (Book 1)
Rescue Me, Cowboy (Book 2)
Complete Me, Cowboy (Book 3)
Sweet Talk Me, Cowboy (Book 4)

Cowboys of Ransom Creek
Her Cowboy Hero (Book 1)
The Cowboy's Bride for Hire (Book 2)
Cooper: Charmed by the Cowboy (Book 3)
Shane: The Cowboy's Junk-Store Princess (Book 4)
Vance: Her Second-Chance Cowboy (Book 5)
Drake: The Cowboy and Maisy Love (Book 6)
Brice: Not Quite Looking for a Family (Book 7)

Texas Matchmaker Series
Dream With Me, Cowboy (Book 1)
Be My Love, Cowboy (Book 2)
This Heart's Yours, Cowboy (Book 3)
Hold Me, Cowboy (Book 4)
Be Mine, Cowboy (Book 5)
Operation: Married by Christmas (Book 6)
Cherish Me, Cowboy (Book 7)
Surprise Me, Cowboy (Book 8)
Serenade Me, Cowboy (Book 9)
Return To Me, Cowboy (Book 10)
Love Me, Cowboy (Book 11)
Ride With Me, Cowboy (Book 12)
Dance With Me, Cowboy (Book 13)

Windswept Bay Series
From This Moment On (Book 1)
Somewhere With You (Book 2)
With This Kiss (Book 3)
Forever and For Always (Book 4)
Holding Out For Love (Book 5)
With This Ring (Book 6)
With This Promise (Book 7)
With This Pledge (Book 8)
With This Wish (Book 9)
With This Forever (Book 10)
With This Vow (Book 11)

About the Author

Bestselling author Debra Clopton has sold over 2.5 million books. Her book OPERATION: MARRIED BY CHRISTMAS has been optioned for an ABC Family Movie. Debra is known for her contemporary, western romances, Texas cowboys and feisty heroines. Sweet romance and humor are always intertwined to make readers smile. A sixth generation Texan she lives with her husband on a ranch deep in the heart of Texas. She loves being contacted by readers.

Visit Debra's website at www.debraclopton.com

Sign up for Debra's newsletter at www.debraclopton.com/contest/

Check out her Facebook at www.facebook.com/debra.clopton.5

Follow her on Twitter at @debraclopton

Contact her at debraclopton@ymail.com

If you enjoyed reading *What Hopes are Made of*, I would appreciate it if you would help others enjoy this book, too.

Recommend it. Please help other readers find this book by recommending it to friends, reader's groups and discussion boards.

Review it. Please tell other readers why you liked this book by reviewing it on the retail site you purchased it from or Goodreads. If you do write a review, please send an email to debraclopton@ymail.com so I can thank you with a personal email. Or visit me at: www.debraclopton.com.

Made in the USA
Coppell, TX
27 October 2021

64758835R00134